The Cats and the Crystal

by

Daniel Steven Kahan

Illustrated by Miranda Mundt

For my parents, who always believed I should publish this story

Table of Contents

I

Runaways

As kittens, Tag and Licorice thought they were just normal cats, living with their parents in a house with a family of people. They had no idea how different they were and what an incredible journey lay ahead of them.

The first sign of things to come took place late one August afternoon when the two brothers were just three months old. In the living room of their comfortable, air-conditioned home, the family of cats relaxed and listened curiously to the T.V. news broadcast. Updates continued about the summer heat wave that was affecting the local area, so the cats were all satisfied to be where they were, safe from the elements or any other danger. Next to the wall and adjacent to the sofa, the cats all sat inside a big old cardboard box that was positioned on its side with the flaps open. The kittens' father, Ralph, had short, black fur, long whiskers, and pale green eyes. Their mother, Daisy, was slender with white fur and emerald green eyes.

Ralph's lengthy whiskers twitched as he looked out of the box. An eight-year-old girl named Penny had, for about the tenth time that day, come to play with Tag and Licorice.

The two kittens purred contentedly as the girl scooped them up and cradled them in her arms. Tag was black all along his tail and back, as well as the upper part of his face. The front of his body, including most of his face, was white. Licorice got his name because of his almost completely black coat. He had only a speck of white on his chest. Both kittens had green eyes like their parents.

Ralph and Daisy knew how lucky they were. They knew that Penny and her parents cared for them and the kittens very much. Three years ago it had been a darker time for them. They had been alley cats, living outdoors, forced to find food for themselves. One day they had come to Penny's house in hopes of receiving a handout, and Penny's family had adopted them. Since then, they had been living a good life.

Penny's mother entered the room and saw her daughter sitting cross-legged in front of the box, cuddling the two kittens. As usual, she wore a professional-looking dress and blouse.

"Well, how are they doing today?" she asked her daughter.

"They're *so cute*," Penny responded, making Tag and Licorice feel proud.

Just then, they all heard the garage door open. Penny and her mother went to greet Mr. Wistingsly, who usually came home from work at about this time. Penny carried the two kittens along with her.

Mr. Wistingsly noisily entered and put down his large, brown briefcase. He was about six feet tall and was wearing a well-tailored suit.

"Hi dear," he said, kissing his wife on the cheek and smiling with an exuberance that was unusual for such a typical workday afternoon. He approached Penny, lifted her up in the air, and spun her around while she still held the kittens. The two kittens giggled with glee, enjoying the free ride and the air rushing past their faces.

Then Mr. Wistingsly kissed his daughter on the cheek and set her down. "Well, I have some good news," he told his family. "Next month, we'll be moving."

At the time, the news meant very little to Tag and Licorice. Their parents, however, looked up with a start as they heard the announcement.

Mr. and Mrs. Wistingsly hugged each other and laughed joyfully, then headed down the hallway, discussing how they would decorate their new home. Penny tagged along also, leaving the two kittens with their parents.

While the kittens returned to their mother, Ralph looked back at her and realized what he should do. Following the people's voices, he proceeded down the hallway to Penny's parents' room, where he quietly peered around the corner. He could see Penny sitting at the edge of the bed, bouncing up and down with enthusiasm at her mother's side. From somewhere out of sight, he could hear Mr. Wistingsly speak.

"I know you'll like the new house, Penny. It has two stories like you've always wanted."

"Is it the one with the swimming pool?" Penny inquired.

"Yep," Mr. Wistingsly answered. "And I think you'll both like Suburb City, too. It has a lot of good restaurants, a movie theater with twenty-eight screens…"

That was all Ralph needed to hear. He rushed back to tell Daisy the bad news.

"You were right! They're moving to Suburb City!"

Tag and Licorice had never seen their father look so distressed.

"What are we going to do?" said Daisy. "We can't go back there!"

Now the two kittens were extremely worried.

"There's only one thing we can do," Ralph said slowly, "— run away with Tag and Licorice!"

A month later, the house looked much different. All the shelves were bare, and there were cardboard boxes everywhere, packed full with books, dishes, pictures, and numerous other items from around the house. The box occupied by the cats was the only empty one. It was the last day before the big move.

It was overcast that morning, and the ground outside was damp. The summer days had turned to autumn, and in the backyard, dewdrops plopped off of the pine trees and onto the thick grass. It was 8:30 A.M., and Penny was already at school. Her mother had left for work two hours ago. Mr. Wistingsly, usually in a rush around this time to get to work by nine, grabbed the umbrella in case it rained and hurried into the garage.

Ralph and Daisy listened carefully as the car engine started. They heard the car pull out and the garage door close.

All was quiet in the house. Ralph and Daisy woke up the sleeping Tag and Licorice.

"Come on, you two," said their mother tenderly. "It's time to go."

The two kittens both yawned and grudgingly opened their eyes. They already knew what was supposed to happen that day.

"Why do we have to leave?" Tag asked.

"Yeah, we like it with the Wistingslys," Licorice complained.

"It's a long story," Ralph told them.

"So? Tell us anyways," said Tag.

Ralph looked at Daisy—it was hard to explain. "The place they're moving to…it's not safe there for cats. We'll explain it to you more when you're older."

The two kittens were so perplexed by their father's answer that they did not know what to say. They just looked at each other blankly.

Ralph coerced the reluctant kittens out of the box. With his two front paws, he then expertly unfastened the collars that had been put around their necks. Tag and Licorice were surprised by their father's ability to remove the collars, but they just assumed that their parents could probably do many things they didn't yet know about.

Ralph and Daisy had already removed their own collars. They knew the tags on the collars would have protected them from being taken to the animal pound, but it was more important that they not be returned to the Wistingslys.

Daisy walked over to the sliding glass door, which led to the backyard, and stood up on her hind legs. Stretching the full length of her body, she handily unlocked the door with her forepaw. She then flipped the small switch at the bottom. Ralph joined her and helped her slide open the heavy, glass door.

Tag and Licorice were astonished. They had never seen their parents do anything like that.

"How did you do that?" Tag asked. Even at his age, he knew that most cats would not be able to open a door that way.

"It's a long story," Ralph told them. "We'll tell you when you're older."

"Why does he keep saying that?" Licorice asked Tag as they headed for the door.

As they walked down the sidewalk, many concerns ran through the parents' minds. Could they find enough food to keep their young kittens alive? Could they stay safe from predators—and what about the animal catcher? They knew that they would face many dangers, but they would protect their kittens any way they could, even if it cost them their own lives. They wished they didn't have to run away, but their alternative—moving to Suburb City—was far more dangerous.

Tag and Licorice did not understand why they had to leave the people that had been caring for them all their lives, but they were excited to be outside for the first time. Everything was new to them—the trees, grass, even cracks in the sidewalk. They looked all around themselves at signs, houses, and parked cars. Every few minutes one of them would stop to examine or smell something, and it was a struggle for their parents to keep them moving. Gradually, the runaway cats journeyed farther from their old home.

By nightfall, the family of cats had arrived at an alley. Cautiously, they entered and had a look around.

There were twelve trashcans, eleven of which were lying sideways. It looked as though there had been a fight recently. Spewed trash lay everywhere. In one corner there was a heap of dirty, ripped clothing. A pungent odor was in the air.

"What are we going to do now?" Licorice glumly said to Tag.

"Be alley cats, I guess," Tag answered back with a sigh.

"This alley is a mess," Daisy declared, "but I don't know if we'll do any better someplace else."

Ralph nodded in agreement.

The four cats took up residence in the alley.

II
Tag, Licorice, and Johnny

It was not long before Tag and Licorice realized that they, too, had abilities like those of their parents. The two kittens could manipulate objects with great ease, and they were able to understand many things from the human world that most animals could not. Since they were very young, though, their abilities were not yet fully developed.

On a few random occasions when a dog or a cat or a wild animal happened to come by the alley, it became obvious to the young kittens that their family's abilities were much different from those of ordinary animals. Their parents already seemed to know that it was useless trying to associate with these animals, but Tag and Licorice were curious enough to try anyways. One time, the kittens encountered a raccoon foraging for food in the alley's trashcans. The two brothers tried to approach it so they could introduce themselves, but the raccoon just snarled at them, swiped at them with its claw, and ran off. After a few encounters like that, the kittens accepted that such attempts were essentially useless. These other animals acted solely on their basic instincts and could not think in more complex ways like the family of cats. Tag and Licorice began to feel excluded from the rest of the world, unable to communicate with anyone besides their own family. The two kittens longed to meet someone else like them and to make some friends.

One day, a month after the cats moved into the alley, Tag and Licorice sat at the curb watching furniture being unloaded from a moving truck and carried into a nearby house. A middle-to-older-aged man, the new owner of the house, stood there on the front lawn holding two young dogs on a leash while he irascibly supervised the movers. The man was extremely critical, yelling and whining dramatically at every little thing the workers did. The two brothers also noticed a small kitten sitting on the house's front steps. Still clinging to the hope that there must be someone else in the world like them, Tag and Licorice were eager to meet the man's animals. The kitten looked over at them and made eye contact.

Three days after the man had moved in, the kitten sneaked out of the house and Tag and Licorice were able to meet him for the first time. An ordinary animal would not have been able to sneak out the way this kitten had—the brothers had gotten their wish.

The kitten's name was Johnny. His eyes were green, and he was mainly gray with some white in front and faint black stripes on his back. Johnny was about as old as Tag and Licorice, but he did not know his exact age. Unlike Tag and Licorice, he had been separated from his parents shortly after he was born.

Johnny's crotchety owner was very cruel and would kick or shove Johnny whenever he was in a bad mood. To make matters worse, the two dogs that lived with Johnny were just regular animals, and they would always bark at him and terrorize him. That was why Johnny preferred to sneak out of the house whenever possible.

Johnny began to visit Tag and Licorice whenever he could, and the three kittens became good friends. Tag and Licorice continued to ask their parents why they and their friend were different from other animals, but their parents still felt that they were too young to understand.

One day, approximately two months after they met, Tag, Licorice, and Johnny came up with a dangerous idea. Instead of playing in the alley like usual, they decided to sneak *into* the man's house and play there. Tag and Licorice knew they shouldn't do it, but they were eager to push the limits of their abilities. They did not tell their parents.

First, the mischievous kittens climbed the tree in the man's backyard and walked out on a branch toward the house. The branch ended a couple of feet away from an open window. From there, Johnny showed Tag and Licorice an opening in the screen that he had made with his claws and teeth. The man had either not noticed it or was too busy to bother repairing it.

"Come on," said Johnny. He turned and readily leaped from the branch onto the windowsill, then slipped through the opening and hopped down into the room.

Tag and Licorice were surprised by the apparent ease with which their friend had accomplished the feat. They timidly stared down at the ground that seemed about a mile below.

"Come on," Johnny urged them again from the room. "You can make it."

The two brothers accepted the challenge. Licorice, who was closest to the window, bent his knees, gathered his nerve, and then sprang across to the other side. Tag then followed suit and made the jump, too, landing next to Licorice on the sill.

The two brothers bounded into the room and looked around. There was a well-made bed, a blue chair, and a pair of dressers. It was the man's bedroom.

Johnny was already at the doorway, peering into the hall, as the two brothers approached to see what he was doing. They stepped back as Johnny then pushed the door closed.

"My owner shouldn't be home for three hours," he told Tag and Licorice, "and this should keep the dogs out—they can't open the door like I can."

"So, what is there to do?" asked Licorice.

Johnny approached the closet. "There's a lot of neat things in here," he answered, sliding the door open and proceeding to scrounge through a box full of miscellaneous items.

"Here's something," he said, handing Licorice a fairly large spring. "And here's this," he added, presenting Tag with a stack of flypaper.

Licorice immediately began playing with the spring, first trying to see how high he could make it bounce, and then trying to bounce himself into the air. Meanwhile, Tag had already gotten stuck to the flypaper, and he rolled around on the floor, playfully struggling to free one paw just as another would get stuck. Johnny laughed with delight at Tag's dilemma and then joined Licorice in playing with the spring.

Suddenly, they all heard a thumping sound—someone was coming up the stairs. Tag and Licorice looked up in alarm.

"Oh no!" cried Johnny. "My owner's coming! What's he doing here?"

"Let's get out of here!" said Licorice, abandoning the spring.

"I'm still stuck!" exclaimed Tag, now desperately trying to remove the flypaper.

Licorice and Johnny approached him so they could help, and soon they all had flypaper stuck to their paws. They could tell that the man had reached the top of the stairs, and they could hear the dogs barking and scratching at the door.

"Use the floor!" Johnny suggested.

They each stuck the flypaper to the floor and used a different paw to hold it down. Then they were able to peel their paws away while the flypaper stayed attached to the carpet.

"Ouch!" yelled Tag as a patch of his fur was torn off.

"Come on!" called Johnny, heading for the window.

The three kittens scampered toward the opening in the screen and hopped up onto the windowsill. Licorice was the first to slip through and leap back outside to the tree, followed by Tag. Johnny went last, and from the safety of the branch, they all looked back and watched as the man entered the room.

"What's going on here?" grumbled the man irritably as the two agitated dogs hustled past him toward the window. "Why was this door closed?" The two dogs started barking at the kittens out in the tree.

"What the—" The man started towards the window, but before he got very far, his foot got caught in the spring that

Licorice had left in the middle of the room. As he started hopping up and down on the other foot, trying to remove the spring, that foot got some flypaper stuck to it. Soon he tumbled to the floor. As the man got up, he began reaching awkwardly for some more flypaper that had gotten stuck to his back. It was almost impossible for him to remove it. From where the kittens were, the scene was hilarious.

The kittens climbed back down the tree and scurried away as fast as they could. By the time they reached a safe place around the side of the house, they had broken out in laughter. Tears streamed down their cheeks from laughing so hard.

That afternoon, after Johnny's owner had gone back to work, Tag, Licorice, and Johnny played tag out in front of the alley. Their spirits were very high; in part because of the incident earlier that day, they were more aware and appreciative of their special abilities. They merrily chased each other every which way while Ralph and Daisy watched vigilantly from a distance.

Suddenly, the cats all heard a car coming. It might have been an ordinary truck to people, but to the animals it meant danger! The alert parents quickly ushered the three kittens into the alley and hushed them.

The truck was from the animal pound. As it passed by, the driver looked every which way but saw nothing.

III
The Animal Catcher

The next day, a little before sunset, Ralph, Daisy, Tag, and Licorice were sitting on the sidewalk outside the alley, eating the meager dinner they had foraged. Once again the two kittens asked their parents about the unique abilities that they and their friend Johnny all possessed. This time, Ralph looked over at Daisy questioningly.

"I think they're old enough now to know," Daisy told him, "especially in case anything ever happens."

"I think so, too," Ralph agreed.

At last, thought Tag and Licorice. They sat up and prepared to hear their father's answer.

"A long time ago—about six years ago," Ralph began, "your mother and I were both born in a secret place called the Animals' Forest. Now, this forest is a very special place because it has several magical properties."

"Magical?" questioned Licorice.

"That's right," Ralph replied. "For one thing, it's called the Animals' Forest because only animals live there. People don't know about it. Somehow, they're just unaware of it, like it doesn't exist."

"Only animals?" repeated Tag skeptically.

"Well, actually," Ralph continued, "they say some people are there, but they're very primitive, like cavemen."

Tag and Licorice listened with fascination.

"Meanwhile, animals who go there gain the types of abilities you've asked us about. And once you've been there, you keep some of those abilities—and it seems your *kittens* get them as well."

Tag and Licorice nodded attentively, knowing that he was referring to them.

"Also, the effects of the Forest extend partially into the surrounding area," added Daisy. "And they decrease the further from the Forest you are."

"So, if we lived in the Forest, we'd have even more abilities," Licorice guessed.

"That's right," Ralph responded.

"What about Johnny?" asked Tag.

"His parents must have lived there, too," answered Daisy.

"The other important thing that you need to know," Ralph went on, "is that, just as people are kept away from it, animals are attracted to it. And from what we've heard, once you've lived there, somehow things will always happen that will make you go back there."

Tag and Licorice looked at each other, not fully understanding.

"Like what kind of things?" inquired Tag.

"Well, for example," Ralph explained, "that's why we ran away. The Wistingslys were going to move to Suburb City, which is the closest city to the Animals' Forest."

"So what's wrong with that?" questioned Licorice. "The Forest sounds like a neat place!"

"It was," Ralph responded sorrowfully, "until King Wolf."

"*King Wolf?*" Tag and Licorice repeated at the same time.

"You see," Ralph continued, "no one used to know about the Animals' Forest, but the people kept cutting down all the trees and building houses and cities. They stopped when they finally reached the Animals' Forest because, as I said, the Forest's magical properties keep them out. But the people's pets—dogs and cats especially—were attracted to the Forest. And once they went in there, they realized how many things they could do…what they could build, how much they could learn…how much they could accomplish. Using materials found in the Forest, and that they acquired in the city, some of them built homes there. Over many generations, their abilities and their technology grew, and the animals built a prosperous kingdom there. Unfortunately, there was one dog named Wolf who wanted to take over the kingdom for himself. He had always felt that dogs were stronger and smarter than other animals and so naturally they should be in charge. Gradually, he recruited other dogs who agreed with his philosophy and eventually he became their king. King Wolf called his army the Canine Order, and they made swords and spears and built a giant fortress called Dog Castle. When I was a kitten, and your mother, too, there was a terrible threat that the Canine Order was going to attack. A lot of young animals, including your mother and I, were taken away from the Forest for their own safety. Our parents all stayed behind to fight the Canine Order, but the cats who took care of us took us to this town and told us all never to go back to the Animals' Forest or Suburb City because it was too dangerous there."

"It was a very sad time," recalled Daisy. "I remember how they decided to stay and fight and how all the kittens and puppies should leave. I remember my sister, Rosie, who was almost a year old. She decided to stay and help our parents, even though she was young enough to leave with the others."

Tag and Licorice looked at each other in amazement as they tried to think of what other questions to ask.

Suddenly, though, the four cats noticed Johnny running frantically toward them. It was peculiar at first—until they realized he was being chased by the two dogs from his house!

"Look out!" Johnny called to them with the dogs still a ways back.

Without even thinking about it, the four cats started running, too, as Johnny caught up with them. They all turned the corner into the alley.

"The trashcan!" Ralph suggested to Daisy, who was closest to the kittens.

Without much time to spare, Daisy directed the kittens into one of the cans that was lying on its side. There was just enough room in front of the foul-smelling garbage for the three of them to squeeze in together. Daisy grabbed the lid from nearby and shoved it in front of the can, along with a few other pieces of rubbish. Then she and Ralph found their own hiding places just as the dogs came around the corner.

The two parents watched nervously from amongst the alley's other debris as the dogs sniffed around thoroughly near the kittens' location. Within the dark container, the three kittens held their breath and tried to remain perfectly still as they heard the dogs panting close by. Fortunately, the stinky trash did a good job of covering up the kittens' scent.

The two dogs searched a while longer, wandering aimlessly about the alley, but were unable to find any trace of the cats. Eventually Johnny's owner came and called the dogs to come home.

The five cats emerged cautiously from the alley and looked around. The dogs and their owner were nowhere in sight.

"What happened, Johnny?" Ralph asked. They could all see that he was shaken up from whatever had just occurred.

"Well, my owner locked me in a room last night—with no food," Johnny explained, "to punish me for what happened yesterday. By today, he still hadn't fed me. I got so hungry—I just had to get out of there. But just when I had finished cutting another hole in the screen of the window, he saw me. I escaped through the window, but he came outside and sent the dogs after me!"

"That's terrible," Daisy sympathized. "What are you going to do now?"

"I don't know…," replied Johnny with tears in his eyes. "All I know is I'm never going back and living in that house again!" He took off his collar and flung it furiously into the alley.

"Well, you're welcome to live with us, Johnny," Daisy kindly told him. The three kittens looked at each other with joyful surprise—it was a wonderful idea.

All of a sudden, seemingly from out of nowhere, a big, long shadow stretched out along the pavement and encompassed the cats, and it became eerily quiet as the low rumbling sound of an automobile engine came to a stop. An animal control truck had pulled up right next to them.

The five cats were taken completely by surprise and scattered in all different directions as the driver got out. Tag ran down the alley while Licorice and Johnny went to opposite sides of it. Daisy took cover behind some trashcans while Ralph had run behind the truck in order to distract the driver from the others.

The man tried to catch Ralph, but cleverly Ralph ducked under the truck and came out on the other side. He scooted over to the trashcans where Daisy waited. The animal catcher then headed toward Johnny, who had not gotten any further away because he had stopped to watch Ralph. The man swung his net at him, but Johnny was able to run between the driver's legs.

Licorice, with so much excitement going on, felt daring and decided to have some fun. After seeing both his father and his friend elude the animal catcher, he approached the man and let the man swing at him. Licorice sprang to the side and the man missed. Then Johnny, realizing that he could avoid the man—and forgetting his recent unpleasant experience with his owner and his dogs—decided to join his friend. Tag then came back and took his chances, too.

The three kittens were not afraid of the animal catcher. With their extraordinary physical abilities, they felt invincible. The man kept swinging the net with more and more determination, and each time one of the agile kittens would duck or leap out of the way. The kittens giggled with reckless exhilaration as the man became more and more frustrated.

"Tag! Licorice! Johnny!" called Daisy urgently. "Get away from there!"

The three kittens heard her, but they were having too much fun to stop now. They continued to push their luck. The man swung and missed again, cursing under his breath.

"Come over here now!" ordered Tag and Licorice's father.

Tag looked up to see where his father was; but the animal catcher, seeing that he was distracted, swung his net. Tag rolled to the side and avoided it, but just as he relaxed, the man swung once more. This time, Tag was too slow and the net went over him. Tag was in shock as he was lifted up into the air within the net. The others watched helplessly.

The back of the truck was a pen enclosed at the rear by wire fencing. The man tilted the the screen upward, tossed Tag in, tilted the screen back down, and closed the latch on the outside. After landing rather roughly in the back of the truck, Tag immediately tried to reopen the latch, but he could not reach far enough between the wires. He tried shaking the screen, but the latch was holding it firmly in place.

Licorice was so dismayed to see his brother get caught that he could not even move. Immediately, the man took another swing at him and scooped him up as well.

Licorice was terrified as he desperately struggled to get free and his limbs got more and more entwined within the net. The animal catcher untangled him and dumped him in the pen with Tag while Ralph, Daisy, and Johnny could only look on in horror. The man opened the screen and closed it much too quickly for Tag to have a chance of getting out.

Then the man was pursuing Daisy, who had come closer to create a diversion. The animal catcher chased after her, but she was too fast for him. She repeatedly eluded the man. Johnny saw Ralph sneaking over to the truck to save Tag and Licorice.

Johnny knew he had to help Ralph. All that was in the way were the animal catcher and his net. He tried to run past as the man took another swing at Daisy, but the man saw him. The animal catcher abandoned Daisy and chased Johnny towards the truck.

Ralph was already trying to pull up the latch, but it was stuck. Johnny jumped up to help him, and together they pulled with all their might. From within the pen, Tag and Licorice saw the animal catcher approaching quickly.

"Look out!" they both cried.

Then the net came down over Johnny. Ralph managed to leap off just in time to avoid capture.

Ralph and Daisy both tried to get the driver's attention so that one of them might still have a chance to open the latch. However, the driver was already exhausted from so much effort. As Johnny squirmed within the net, the man stood there with his hands on his knees, trying to catch his breath.

"That's a nice catch," he said to himself.

After throwing Johnny in—again too fast for the others to get out—he snapped a padlock in place on the latch. Then he got into the truck and started the engine. A puff of black smoke coughed out from the exhaust pipe, and the vehicle began to pull away.

Ralph and Daisy chased after it for as long as they could, but eventually they could not keep up. They watched in despair as the truck disappeared from their sight.

Tag and Licorice grasped the fence at the back of the truck. They were too stunned to do or say anything. They just watched as their parents got farther and farther away.

Meanwhile, Ralph and Daisy wondered if they would ever see Tag or Licorice again, but they knew they would start a search for their kittens. They would search until they found them no matter what it took.

Johnny tried to console Tag and Licorice as they cried on their way to wherever they were being taken. It had been a sad day for them all.

IV
Suburb City

The next few days for the kittens were long and dismal. They were each confined in their own individual travel cage, and along with other unfortunate animals, transported from place to place in the dark, stuffy backs of trucks. The cages would slide around when the trucks were moving and would vibrate or shift suddenly whenever the trucks went over bumps in the road. At night the kittens were housed with numerous other animals in bleak, unfamiliar storage buildings, and then in the morning, they would be loaded back into another truck. Tag, Licorice, and Johnny had no idea how far they had traveled when finally they arrived at their destination—a pet shop.

The place had an attractive, red neon sign on display in front with the name "Pat's Pets" in fancy handwriting. Pat's Pets was one of several pet stores in the area that accepted strays and sold them to new owners.

While the animals waited in their cages for the workers to prepare a space for them, they observed their new surroundings. There were birds, cats, dogs, fish, hamsters, lizards, turtles, and many other animals for sale. A large variety of equipment for the pets, such as leashes, fish tanks, and hamster cages, was available, and one of the store's main attractions seemed to be a particularly large selection of toys. Various people were venturing in and out through the front door, and a little jingle was heard each time someone did. From the amount of business going on at the time, Pat's Pets seemed to be a popular place.

As the three friends were released from their travel cages into their new home in a large, clear plastic cage on a shelf, they immediately noticed the unruly behavior of the other kittens in the enclosure. Some were crowding around the edges of the pen, yelling at their captors and pleading for their freedom.

"Hey, let us out of here!"

"Please! We don't belong here!"

Others were getting used to their surroundings.

"What kind of place is this?"

"Hey, this place smells."

Still others were too young to truly realize their predicament and just seemed glad to be out of the travel cages. They chased each other around obliviously within the small confines of the pen.

The three friends just looked at each other, realizing…these kittens were just like them!

Over the next few days, Tag, Licorice, and Johnny made friends with the other kittens. They were glad to have finally met some other animals like themselves, but they wished it could have happened someplace other than in captivity. Tag and Licorice shared the story their parents had told them about why they had different abilities apart from other animals, and surely enough, some of the others had been told the same thing. Many of the kittens also had parents or other family members who had once lived in Suburb City or the Animals' Forest, and several of them had also been warned to stay away from there. From the kittens' observations of the other animals in the store, it was evident that every animal in the place was like them.

Tag, Licorice, and Johnny soon discovered the reason why the other animals were like them—they were, indeed, in Suburb City. As Ralph and Daisy had described, a series of events had occurred, which, as if by chance, had brought them there. Since they were imprisoned there in the cage, though, there was nothing they could do about it.

As the days went by, Tag and Licorice eventually came to accept that they would probably never see their parents again. Instead, they each knew that if anyone bought them, they would have to run away, leave Suburb City, and become alley cats again—even if it meant they would not see each other again either. Johnny, who had never heard about Suburb City or the Canine Order before coming to the pet shop, realized the same thing. Many of the kittens, however, seemed less concerned about the story and just hoped to find a nice home.

One day, an attractive young woman entered the pet store. She was dressed casually, wearing blue jeans and a white, button-down shirt.

"I'm looking for a cat," she told the salesperson in a pleasant voice.

Immediately most of the kittens looked up with enthusiasm, as they usually did whenever there was a chance of being bought.

"What kind of cat are you looking for?" the clerk inquired, seeming especially attentive.

"It doesn't matter," the woman told him. "Just something small—I need to feed it to my pet snake."

Tag, Licorice, and Johnny looked at each other, aghast—had they heard her correctly? The other kittens seemed stunned as well, and some of them started trembling. Some of them huddled together as if they could protect each other somehow.

"What'd she say?" said one kitten, who had been half asleep.

The clerk was taken aback at first, but proceeded to lead the woman past the cages of some of the other, older cats. The two of them stopped in front of the kittens' cage, and the woman eyed Johnny closely.

"He's a little *too* small," she said dismissively.

Johnny breathed a sigh of relief.

The woman's stare moved along past some of the others until she focused on Licorice. Licorice paced back and forth nervously in the cage.

"Too thin."

Licorice looked at Johnny thankfully.

Then the woman saw Tag. "This one will be good," she told the clerk.

Tag was terrified, but he knew what he had to do. Licorice and Johnny held their breath as the clerk opened up the cage.

Suddenly, Tag leaped out through the opening and onto the floor. He ran for the door of the pet shop, but another salesperson scooped him up. Tag desperately wriggled and twisted to free himself.

"Actually," said the woman, "maybe he's a little too feisty."

The second clerk brought Tag back to the cage, and Tag gratefully leaped back in and pulled the door shut himself.

The woman was as picky as she was eccentric. Eventually, she could not find any suitable cat and left with nothing.

It was December, and many animals including the kittens had their prices lowered for a holiday sale. Many joyful things seemed to be going on everywhere. The three kittens learned about the holiday season and did not want to spend it cooped up in a pet shop.

Two days before Christmas, a long, black limousine pulled up outside the store, and an old lady wearing very elegant clothing emerged from the back of the vehicle. She had grayish-white hair and blue eyes, and she walked with a cane. The lady entered the pet shop.

The lady seemed quite pleasant as she spoke to the salespeople. She looked at various animals but gradually made her way to the cat section. With high hopes, Tag, Licorice, Johnny, and all the others stood on their hind legs and leaned against the clear walls of the cage. The lady looked at Johnny.

"I'd like this kitten here," she told the clerk in a dear voice.

While the clerk escorted the lady to the register, Tag, Licorice, and Johnny sadly said their goodbyes. They had all known that this day would come eventually.

The people returned to the cage, and the clerk opened it. Johnny jumped into the woman's arms with glee, and the old lady giggled with joy as she received her new kitten. While Johnny was ecstatic to finally be freed from captivity, he was sorry to be leaving Tag and Licorice. As the lady carried him off, he looked back and waved goodbye to his best friends. He knew he would probably never see them again.

Tag and Licorice waved back and watched as the lady and Johnny got into the limousine. All the brothers had now was each other, and they knew that any day they might be separated, too.

That night, Johnny lay down by a crackling fire in a luxurious mansion. Trying to forget about his old friends, he fell asleep.

Eventually he had a nightmare. He dreamt that an evil wizard took a maze out of a book and made it real. The wizard threw Tag and Licorice in. Johnny, himself, was in a house, nice and warm, yet he could see them suffering, trapped and lost inside the maze. He never saw what happened to Tag and Licorice.

Johnny woke up around 5:00 A.M., horrified. He knew what he had to do that day.

Later, when the lady had woken up, Johnny tried to tell her that he wanted some cats for friends. He had never had much luck communicating with his previous owner, but he knew he had to try. Using a mirror and a series of meows, Johnny tried several times to explain his message. He repeated it over and over again until, amazingly, the lady understood, except she assumed he meant one cat.

In the pet shop, Tag and Licorice were curled up next to each other, trying to keep warm. Amidst the other kittens running blithely about the cage, they gazed out at the street and observed in silent contemplation the tiny snowflakes wafting delicately to the ground. The brothers perked up as they noticed a familiar limousine parking in front of the store. An unexpected face appeared at the store's entrance.

The lady carried Johnny with her directly to the cat section, and the kittens, including Tag and Licorice, once again crowded against the clear walls of the cage. Johnny motioned excitedly to the whole group, hoping that maybe, since the lady was quite wealthy, she might buy *all* the kittens.

"Well, which one does kitty want?" asked the lady, trying to understand.

Johnny kept pointing vigorously.

"Oh, I don't think I can take care of that many kitties," said the lady. "You'll have to pick just one."

Johnny realized he could never convince her to buy all the kittens, but he couldn't choose between Tag and Licorice. He pointed back and forth earnestly to both of them.

"Okay, kitty can have two friends," the lady decided.

Johnny nodded happily in agreement, and Tag and Licorice were bought and reunited with their friend. They were all sorry to leave the other kittens behind, but they knew there was nothing more they could do. The lady took the three of them home to her mansion.

Later, Johnny explained to Tag and Licorice how he been able to convey to the lady his desire for her to return to the pet shop. Apparently, the friends realized, the magic from the Animals' Forest was strong in Suburb City, and it had helped him communicate.

Unfortunately, the cats knew that they couldn't stay. They had to get out of Suburb City as soon as possible. They decided, however, to first stay for the night and get a good night's sleep. At least it seemed safe enough there in the mansion. The next day they would leave.

That night, the three kittens slept well in front of the fireplace in the lady's mansion. They were glad to be together again.

In the morning, the three kittens woke up to find several ornately wrapped packages under the lady's Christmas tree. It was then that they realized it was Christmas Day.

The kittens bounded over to the gifts. On each of the presents was a card that read: "To Kitties."

The three kittens tore open the wrapping on the presents. They had received a big, red, white, and blue beach ball; a basketball; two soccer balls; a tennis ball; and a dark blue, vinyl gym bag that held thirty black and blue rubber balls. The three kittens were delighted.

"Was Santa Claus good to you?" asked the lady from the top of the stairs. The kittens shook their heads up and down with enthusiasm.

Although the cats had planned to leave, they decided to stay for a little while to play with their gifts. There was no way they could take the balls with them.

Eventually the cats decided to remain with the old lady. She had already been so kind to them that they would feel bad about running away. Also, they knew it was unlikely that they would ever find a better home than this one. Besides, there didn't *seem* to be any danger, as long as they were with the lady.

As the days went by, the three cats' abilities grew considerably, and they became more capable of communicating with the old lady. Sometimes the lady would cough badly or get tired easily, which worried the cats. Because of the lady's fragile health, they made certain to help her around the house whenever possible.

The lady was more than just an owner to Tag, Licorice, and Johnny. She spent as much time with them as she could, read to them, and even cooked meals for the three cats. Since she lived alone and had no close relatives, they were her only family. The three cats loved her, and she loved them. They all lived in the big mansion happily.

As they got older, the three cats began to spend some time outside of the house. They never went far, though, because they were still concerned about the story Tag and Licorice's parents had told about Suburb City.

One day in the middle of March, Tag, Licorice, and Johnny were playing at the end of the block, as they often did. Tag passed the tennis ball to Licorice. Licorice passed it back to Tag. Tag faked a throw, and Johnny leaped up into the air. Right when Johnny landed, Tag threw it back to Licorice. They were playing keep away.

On one of Tag's throws, Johnny tipped it. The ball went rolling into an alley that was filled with soot, and the three cats jumped in after it. Licorice found the ball, but the cats decided to play in the soot for a while.

Later when they emerged from the alley, the three cats were filthy. They were so caught up in talking and laughing that before they realized it, they had wandered next to a group of five men—who appeared to be drunk. One of the men spoke.

"Well, look what we have here—some cats."

"They must be alley cats—they're so dirty," said another.

"Let's take'em to the boss!"

The three cats knew they had just walked into trouble. They looked urgently for a path of escape, but the men already had them surrounded. A few of the men reached down to pick them up.

After their previous experience with the animal catcher, the three cats were nearly petrified. The men got a hold of Tag and Johnny, but Licorice managed to squirm his way free. The men ignored Licorice once he got a few feet away, but they started to walk away with Tag and Johnny.

"Tag! Johnny!" yelled Licorice as he followed them, but it was no use. Tag and Johnny kept struggling madly but in vain.

The men continued laughing and joking with each other as they carried the cats across the street. They disappeared through a servants' entrance at the side of the mansion there.

Licorice rushed back inside the house and frantically tried to tell the lady what had just happened. Because he was so agitated, it was quite difficult for her to understand him. Eventually, though, she carried Licorice with her across the street.

When a servant answered the door, the lady tried to explain that people from there had taken her two cats. Unfortunately, the servant had no idea what the drunken men had done and refused to interrupt his employer for something so "petty."

The lady returned twice the next day but was met only with rudeness. For whatever reason, the servants were unwilling to let her talk to their employer.

Because the people across the street were so uncooperative, the lady called the police. Two officers came and joined the lady in confronting her neighbor. The servants refused to let the police in! The officers told the lady that the only way they could legally enter her neighbor's house would be to obtain a warrant from a judge. Unfortunately, that would never happen for an accusation as minor as the theft of two cats. The lady filed a lawsuit against her neighbor across the street, but as her lawyer pointed out, it would take a very long time to resolve the issue. There was nothing more the lady could do.

V
Softy and the Boss

For a whole week, Licorice did nothing but stay inside and mope around the house. He kept hoping that Tag and Johnny would find a way to sneak away from the people who had taken them, but each day it became more evident that they were unable to do so.

In the mansion across the street, Tag and Johnny knew about the lawsuit that had been filed, so they knew the lady was trying to get them back. Unfortunately, the people there either didn't care about the lawsuit or were just too stubborn to return them.

The two cats shared a tiny room as their personal quarters. The room was filled with plush pillows in an assortment of colors, and they each had a cot on which to sleep. They missed Licorice as much as he missed them.

Much different from the lady's home, this mansion was a very busy place, crawling with servants and security guards. Phones were ringing all the time, and people in suits would hurry in every direction with briefcases and papers. Business was conducted at all hours of the day.

"Call the agency!"

"It needs to be delivered by tomorrow!"

"How much does it cost?"

What Tag and Johnny really wondered about was the central figure of all the people there, a middle-aged man conceited enough to sit on a gold throne in the large room outside theirs. The cats did not know the man's real name, so they just called him "the boss." That was what everyone else called him.

Actually, the boss paid very little attention to the two cats. It seemed that all he cared about were his gold, silver, and platinum mines; his stocks and bonds; and his other business ventures. Much of the time he was on the phone talking to his agents. He would gesture proudly to his vault, which spanned nearly the entire wall at the end of the room. Most of the time, the huge, metal door was left open so that everyone could admire the boss's enormous collection of treasure chests, gold coins, precious jewels, and cash.

Tag and Johnny did not understand why the boss even kept them. They seemed to be just two very minor items amongst his vast wealth; but, as they had already learned, the boss never parted with *any* of his wealth. The cats were treated well enough, but they were miserable anyways. There was nothing to do, and they weren't allowed to venture any further than the boss's chamber. They had tried to escape a few times already, but each time the security guards had grabbed them or ushered them back to their room. Despite the cats' intelligence and exceptional abilities, people still had control over them.

After a week of sulking, Licorice finally decided that he had to do something. If Tag and Johnny could not get to him, he thought, maybe he could go to them and free them somehow.

One evening, he crept outside without the lady's knowledge. Across the street, several elegant automobiles—mostly limousines—were being parked, and various well-dressed, important-looking people were being welcomed into the mansion.

Licorice crossed the street and slipped through the bars of the other mansion's wrought-iron fence. He made his way to an open window at the side of the household and jumped up on the windowsill. Peering inside, he could see an empty dining room with a long table. As Johnny had once described to him, he started cutting into the screen with his claws. Before long, he was able to bend down a flap in the screen and poke his head through.

Just as he was about to enter the room, three maids walked in and started setting the table. Thinking fast, he leaped down inside and ran underneath the table without being seen. He then flitted behind the maids and slinked down a long hallway. Trying to guess which way to go, he peaked around the corner into a pantry area. There were a number of shelves filled with foodstuffs and dishware.

Suddenly he heard a high-pitched shriek that only an animal could hear. Glancing into the corner nearest to him, he saw a tiny mouse with its leg ensnared in a mousetrap. As Licorice observed the frightened creature's expression, he realized it wasn't the trap that had made the creature shriek; it was because the mouse had seen him, a cat, coming around the corner.

Remembering very well how terrified he'd felt when he was caught by the animal catcher, Licorice felt compassion for the mouse. He tried to approach him in a friendly manner.

The little mouse was trembling. He had thick, silky, gray fur.

"Take it easy," said Licorice, trying to calm him. "I'm going to get you out of there."

"That would be awfully nice of you," squeaked the captive mouse, "but if you're just doing it so you can eat me, I'd rather you just left me in the trap."

"Don't worry," Licorice assured him as he slowly reached out his paw.

The mouse didn't seem convinced, recoiling terribly as the paw came toward him, but Licorice bent back the thick, metal wire that had been pressed tightly against the mouse's hind leg. Taking a few fragile steps forward, the mouse was free, and Licorice let the metal snap back down against the wood.

"Thanks," said the mouse. "I needed that."

"You're welcome," Licorice replied as it occurred to him to ask if the mouse had seen Tag and Johnny. Unfortunately, they both heard footsteps coming down the hall.

Licorice and the mouse crouched in the corner as the three maids hurried past them and started gathering dishes for the table. They had not yet noticed the two animals.

"Oh no!" said the mouse. "If they see me, they're going to hit me with a broom!" Instinctively the little mouse tried to run, but the trap had wounded his leg, and all he could do was limp. There was no way he could get very far.

Licorice knew he could sneak past the maids and continue his search for Tag and Johnny, but he couldn't just leave the poor mouse at the mercy of the people there.

"Grab onto my fur," he instructed the mouse. "We're getting out of here." He reached out his paw for the mouse to climb on, but the mouse automatically drew back from him.

"Are you sure you're not going to try to eat me?" he asked nervously.

"Sure I'm sure," answered Licorice. "I can get all the food I want from my owner."

Feeling reassured, the injured mouse accepted his offer. Starting from Licorice's left front paw, he climbed up the cat's leg and struggled his way up to his shoulder.

Once the mouse had a hold of his fur, Licorice left the pantry and ran back up the long hallway. Hastily he turned into the dining area where he was noticed immediately by several of the guests who had just arrived. With them was the boss.

"Hey! How'd that animal get in here?" he demanded with embarrassment and dismay.

Numerous people came rushing toward Licorice as he darted under the table. He ran all the way to the other end, hoping to reach the window, but when he got there, one servant happened to be blocking the way. Licorice skidded to a stop at the man's feet and, just as the man reached down for him, jumped up onto the table. Another servant tried to grab him from the side, but Licorice sprang away from him and ran back across the dinner table. As one of the maids tried to reach him, he leaped off the table and onto a serving cart, upsetting several plates and spilling a bowl of salad.

By now, all the guests were talking and pointing, and the room was in a general state of disorder. The boss was busy trying to explain how this sort of thing had never happened before. Licorice jumped down to the floor, and the frenzied servants chased him every which way until he ducked back under the table. With the terrified mouse hanging on for dear life, he raced across and came out near the window again. This time, the way was clear.

As several people converged on him, he leaped up to the window, bent down the flap in the screen, and slipped through.

Outside, there was a security guard who had heard the ruckus and come to the window. He chased after the two animals, but Licorice was much too fast for him.

"Keep off the boss's property, you mangy cat!" both animals heard as Licorice scampered across the boss's lawn.

On the sidewalk in front of Licorice's home, the two animals introduced themselves.

"My name's Licorice. What's yours?" said Licorice.

"Softy," the mouse answered.

"You must have gotten that name because of your fur," Licorice supposed. He reached out and petted the mouse's soft fur. After their escape from the mansion, the mouse no longer seemed afraid of him.

"And I can understand where you got your name," said Softy. "Your fur is all black—except for that white spot on your chest."

"I guess so," said Licorice, who really had no idea what that had to do with his name. "So, what were you doing in that awful place?" he asked.

"I thought it would be good living there," Softy explained, "because there were so many people and so many guests and there were always a lot of scraps of food for me. Pretty soon, though, they found out I was there and didn't want me to be there, so they started setting traps. Of course, they didn't realize that I knew how the traps worked, and I could easily take the food from the traps without getting caught. Unfortunately, this time when I took the food, I turned and it snapped on my tail. I tried to lift up the metal, but I wasn't strong enough. So I tried using all four legs, and I was barely able to lift it a little bit, but when I got my tail out, it came down on my leg. So then I was stuck. It's a good thing you came when you did, or I'd've been finished for sure!"

Licorice was not surprised that Softy understood how the mousetraps worked. Though he, Tag, and Johnny had yet to meet anymore animals after those in the pet shop, they had suspected that others in the city would have the same abilities as them.

"Well, I guess I'd better get going and try to find a new home," said Softy. "Thanks again for getting me out of there—and out of that nasty mousetrap."

"What about your leg?" questioned Licorice. "It might be broken."

"It'll be okay," the mouse assured him as he started to walk, with difficulty, down the pavement. "Thanks again."

"Don't mention it," Licorice replied sadly, sorry to see the little mouse leaving so soon. It had been nice to have another animal to talk to, even if only for a brief time. Then he had an idea. "Why don't you come see my owner?" he offered, pointing to the mansion where he lived. "She's really nice. Maybe she can help you."

"Most people don't like having mice in their houses," Softy informed the naïve cat, who obviously did not know about such things.

"But *my* owner is different," Licorice insisted. "I'm sure she would help you."

Softy sighed. Although he was scared to death of people, he also knew that he might not survive for long in his present condition...and Licorice had not let him down so far. "Okay...," he agreed timidly. "You're the nicest cat I ever met," he added gratefully.

Licorice almost blushed. He felt kind of embarrassed.

Licorice took the mouse back home with him and brought him to the old lady. While the lady was surprised and a bit uncertain at first, she proved to be as compassionate as Licorice had expected.

The next morning, the lady took the two animals in her limousine to the veterinarian. The vet examined Softy's leg and determined that it was only sprained. The swelling had already diminished significantly overnight. Softy left the animal hospital with a clean bill of health.

The lady and the two animals returned home to the mansion. Licorice had asked if Softy could stay with them, and the lady had agreed that it was okay, as long as there was only one mouse and he was Licorice's responsibility.

As Licorice and Softy entered the living room, Licorice saw all of the cats' toys scattered about, just where they had sat all week. Although he was glad to have helped Softy, he wished he hadn't been forced to abandon his quest the previous night. Trying again to find Tag and Johnny would be difficult; the people across the street would be ready for him. Faced with this realization, he instantly returned to the hopeless, sad state he had been in for days.

At the same time, Softy noticed the cats' bag of rubber balls. He scurried over to it and hopped inside. "Can I sleep in here?" he asked. "It's perfect."

Licorice shrugged. "If you want to…I don't care."

Softy was about to playfully dive down amongst the rubber balls, but he sensed Licorice's sudden change of mood. "What's wrong?" he inquired.

"Oh…nothing," replied Licorice.

"Are you sure?" the mouse replied. After a moment's thought, he smartly asked, "What were you doing last night in the house across the street?"

Licorice decided that he might as well tell him. "My brother and my friend were captured by some men from over there. They grabbed them after we were playing in the alley. I was trying to find them."

"Gee…," said Softy. "That's sad. What are their names?"

"Tag and Johnny."

"Which one is your brother?"

"Tag."

"Is there anything I can do to help you?" offered Softy.

"I don't think so," answered Licorice gloomily.

"You wouldn't have gotten to them that way," Softy told him. "They're all the way in the back, and you were near the front."

Licorice perked up. "You know where they are?" he asked.

"There's two cats right next to the boss's chamber. At first I thought you were one of them. I stayed away from them *and* the boss as much as I could."

"The *boss*?" said Licorice inquisitively.

Softy did not answer at first. He seemed to be thinking about something.

"Never mind about that," he said at last. "But I know how to get your friends out of there."

"How?" Licorice asked eagerly.

Softy described to Licorice a hole in the side of the boss's mansion through which he had originally entered the property. The hole had been caused by water damage from one of the mansion's pipes, and no one seemed to know about it. Although the hole was only big enough for a mouse, Softy was certain that Tag and Johnny would be strong enough to break through some of the brittle material. The hole led to the mansion's cellar, and from the cellar, a flight of stairs led up into the mansion, not far from the boss's chamber. Softy would go back into the mansion, sneak past the guards, and show Tag and Johnny the way out.

Licorice liked the idea, but then he was uncertain. "It's too risky," he told the mouse. "What if they catch you? And what about your leg? I should be the one to go."

"You're too big," replied Softy. "They'll catch you. But they won't catch me because I'm too small. And my leg is much better now. Besides, you were nice to me—now I want to help you."

Late that night, Licorice and Softy stood at the curb in front of the lady's mansion.

"Don't get caught in any mousetraps," Licorice advised his new friend.

"You don't need to remind me," Softy replied.

Then the intrepid mouse headed across the street. He sneaked onto the boss's property and entered the dark hole at the side of the house.

Softy knew the way very well. He adeptly climbed down some shelves into the mansion's cellar and then quickly made his way up the stairs. The door at the top was closed, but he knew that sooner or later somebody would come down to retrieve some of the boss's favorite wine or something else that was stored down there.

After waiting only ten minutes, crouched against the top step, Softy alertly slipped through the door as a servant hurriedly came down the stairs. Hiding behind desks, chairs, and other furniture, the mouse made his way through the mansion. He soon sneaked up to the entryway of a large room.

Judging by the golden throne in the room, Softy knew he was in the right place. Although it was late, there were several people present, including the boss, all quite busy. There were two security guards standing just inside the doorway, but they were distracted, talking to a young lady. Across that room was another, smaller, room filled with pillows.

Softy knew it was the cats' room. He just had to sneak across, but there was no way to do so without being out in the open…

Softy knew what he had to do. Observing the people's activities and waiting for just the right moment, the tiny mouse got ready and then boldly sprinted across the room.

The boss just barely noticed something out of the corner of his eye, but he was unsure. With a mere wave of his finger, he summoned the two guards from the doorway, and the men approached.

"I thought I saw a mouse run by," the boss said crossly. "Find him and get rid of him. I don't want this place to get overrun by rodents."

Meanwhile, Softy had entered Tag and Johnny's room and found the two cats nestled amongst all the colorful pillows. "Are you guys Tag and Johnny?" he asked, approaching Tag.

"Yes," Tag answered curiously.

"I'm here to help you. I know how you can get out of here."

Just then, the pair of guards entered to inspect the cats' room. With alert thinking—and to Softy's dismay—Tag reached out and pulled the mouse towards him, hiding him under his belly. The two cats looked up innocently.

The guards hastily tossed the pillows every which way— ruining the arrangement the cats had made—and then left.

Tag stood up and Softy emerged, panting heavily and spitting out some strands of cat hair. "It's hot under there!" he declared. Then he explained how they could all escape through the cellar.

"We should wait until later," Johnny proposed, "when the boss and most of the guards go to sleep."

Back outside, Licorice waited anxiously for Softy to return, hopefully with Tag and Johnny, but he hadn't realized how long it would take. Eventually it got very late and he went inside. Even later, he fell asleep. When he awoke the next morning, he realized that not only were Tag and Johnny not there, but Softy had not come back either. Now he became extremely worried.

For the whole day Licorice was restless. Had Softy been caught? The evening came again, and still the mouse had not returned.

Licorice felt terrible. He had sent the poor little mouse on a hopeless mission. He couldn't bear to think of what the boss's people had done to him.

Licorice tried to stay up late again that night. He sat crouched by the sliding glass door at the back of the house, the one he, Tag, and Johnny typically used. Eventually, though, he just couldn't keep his eyes open. He rested his head on his paws for just a second and started dreaming that he was in the boss's dining room, being chased. Suddenly, he felt someone tap him on the back. He let out a small yelp and turned, ready to fight. Then he saw that it was Tag! Johnny stood behind him, and Softy was with them!

Licorice was overjoyed to see his brother and his friends again, but he was also curious. After hugging all of them, he asked, "What took you so long?"

"The boss had exterminators searching for Softy all last night," Tag explained. "We had to wait until tonight."

"Softy distracted the guards," Johnny added, "and that helped us get out of the boss's chamber. Once we reached the cellar, we were home free."

That night was a happy one. The next day the lady discovered that Tag and Johnny were back. She had no idea how they had escaped, but they were all glad to be together again.

After that day, Softy and the three cats became the best of friends. The lady canceled the lawsuit.

VI
"The Rich Cats"

Tag, Licorice, and Johnny were the lady's dearest and only friends. She was a widow, and she had no other family. The three cats enjoyed living with her for several more months, but at the end of June, the lady passed away.

The three cats and Softy were very sad. They could not imagine that they would ever encounter another person who would care for them so much. The lady had saved the cats from captivity, taken them into her home, and treated them as family. Because the cats had been able to communicate with her, their relationship had been that much more special. The lady's chauffer took the cats to attend her funeral.

The funeral was very small and simple, especially for such a wealthy person. Because the lady did not have many connections, there were only a few people who attended, and the motivation of some of them was quite clear—they hoped to be left with some of the lady's money.

When they returned to the mansion, a few people convened in the living room for the reading of the lady's will. The cats were rather nervous, wondering what would happen to them. Would they be bequeathed to another person, along with all the lady's possessions? Would the people perhaps try to send them back to the pet shop? Worse yet, would they be thrown out in the street, without the security of their home or anyone to feed them? As the lady's lawyer read the will, though, everyone was surprised to find out that she had left all her money, property, and possessions to...*the three cats!* The three cats looked at each other in disbelief, as did all the people in the room.

The lady's lawyer was very loyal to her and followed her instructions precisely. In particular, he had made certain provisions for taking care of the property that would make it legal for the cats to stay there. The limousine driver quit because he did not want the job of driving three cats around. The animals now lived alone in the mansion.

In spite of the sudden fortune they had acquired, though, all the cats really wished was that the lady could still be with them. They knew that everything she owned had already belonged to them anyways. The cats mourned for their owner whom they had so dearly loved.

Long ago the lady had realized how smart Tag, Licorice, and Johnny were. To make it possible for the cats to live alone, she had moved all of her money to a single safe located within the mansion. The cats knew the combination to the safe, as the lady had shared it with them many times, evidently so they could use it after she was gone.

As the three cats got older, their abilities increased dramatically. They were already over one year old, and it was easy for them to take care of themselves. With the vast supply of cash at their disposal, they learned quickly enough to go into town and communicate with people to buy food or other items. They soon discovered that all animals in the city shared the same abilities as them, and the citizens were quite used to it.

The cats had already learned from the lady that it was not uncommon in Suburb City for unusual things to happen to cats, dogs, and other animals. However, it was quite extraordinary for any animal to inherit a person's home. After Tag, Licorice, and Johnny became heirs to all of the lady's assets, they were visited by numerous reporters and camera crews. For the first few weeks it seemed that whenever they went outside or looked out the window, there was a newsperson or a photographer there.

The cats were not quite sure how to deal with all the attention. At first they would try to avoid being photographed or filmed, but after a while they learned to just ignore all the fuss. Eventually the reporters stopped coming, but not until the cats had already been shown on television and all over the Internet. They had already come to be known as "the rich cats."

Tag, Licorice, and Johnny began to spend more time in the city and found that it was home to quite a large, diverse population of animals, consisting primarily of cats and dogs but also including parrots, canaries, and other birds; snakes, turtles, and other reptiles; frogs, toads, and other amphibians; as well as gerbils, hamsters, mice, rats, ferrets, rabbits, pot-bellied pigs, horses, and other mammals. The large number of animals was almost certainly due to the city's proximity to the Animals' Forest. Many of them lived in homes with people, taking advantage of the comfortable environments provided by their owners; others preferred the independence of living on their own. Similar to Tag, Licorice, and Johnny, most of the city's animals were well-equipped with the skills necessary to survive without the aid of people.

The three cats remembered Ralph and Daisy's warning about Suburb City, but there didn't seem to be any problems. The only effect from what had once happened in the Animals' Forest seemed to be a lingering unease between the cats and dogs of the city. Even though most of the city's dogs had never supported King Wolf—or even seen him—some of the cats felt a sense of distrust towards them because of what King Wolf's Canine Order had done. In particular, it was rumored that King Wolf had agents in the city whose job it was to gather information about the cats, and no one could tell who they might be except that they were dogs. As a result, some cats treated all dogs with suspicion and tended not to associate with them much. In return, the dogs—who despised King Wolf as much as anyone—had formed their own social circles apart from the cats.

Since they were famous, it was not long before the three cats were able to meet many of the city's animals, including a few dogs. Some animals were jealous of them because of their wealth and their fame, but others soon became good friends of the three cats.

One day, Tag, Licorice, and Johnny met three female cats, whom they asked on a triple date. Tag's date was named Mandy; Licorice's date was named Mary; and Johnny's date was named April. They met later that day at a place called the Cougar Club Coffee Shop.

The Coffee Shop was, in fact, an alley that served as a restaurant for animals. All animals were welcome there, but it was most popular amongst the cats.

There were five cats in charge of the shop. Every morning they would get leftover food from a friendly man who owned a store next to the alley. They would pour water from a hose near the back door of one of the adjacent buildings and procure other various types of food from wherever they could.

When Tag, Licorice, and Johnny arrived, they saw many cats inside. There were broken-down bench-tables to sit on and a broken-down piano next to a large wooden plank, which was used as a stage for entertainment. One of the cats in charge named Lenny was hard at work playing a lively tune on the piano. A "chef," the head of the restaurant, and his assistant could be seen in the "kitchen," an area surrounded by crates, where they were busy pouring water and preparing food for the customers. The other two cats were moving from table to table, serving as waiters. This was the most popular place in the city for cats to gather socially.

As Tag, Licorice, and Johnny entered, they greeted many of their friends and acquaintances who happened to be present. Other cats observed them from afar, recognizing them as the rich cats.

Soon they found their dates. Mandy had pale yellow-green eyes and charcoal gray fur with almost a blue tint; she wore a blue bow on her tail. Mary's eyes were sky blue, and her fur was white with some gray around her face and the tips of her ears; she wore a purple bow. April had amber-colored eyes and was mostly white with some black and orange patches; she wore an orange bow.

One of the waiters showed the six cats to a table. They sat down and ordered some water.

Unfortunately, the three bullies, Tiger, Toger, and Tugger, were also there, loitering beside the piano. All three of them were orange and white with black stripes and yellow eyes. Everyone assumed they were brothers because of their similar names, but no one knew for sure. They were all fairly large, for cats. As soon as they noticed the three rich cats, they made a point of strolling over to their table.

"Oh no," said Mandy as they approached. "Look who's here."

"Well, what do we have here?" said Tiger, in his usual loud voice. "It's the '*rich* cats'."

"No one invited you over here, Tiger," Mandy told him.

"I wonder why they're *here*," said Toger, ignoring her, "when they could be home in their *mansion*."

Johnny could feel the fur on the back of his neck standing up as he began to feel tense. He hadn't felt this way since his original owner's dogs had used to corner him and bark and intimidate him.

"Just ignore them," Mary advised Tag, Licorice, and Johnny.

"Yeah, they're not worth the trouble," April said tartly.

"I think they'd better go back home right *now*," said Tugger threateningly.

The three bullies were standing extremely close now.

"We—" started Tag.

"I don't think so," interrupted Johnny, startling Tag and Licorice.

Tugger took Johnny's defiant tone as a challenge. "Well *I* do," he replied, giving Johnny a shove that caused him to lose his balance and almost fall from his seat.

Johnny reacted by standing up and trying to push Tugger, but the bully pushed him first, knocking him to the ground. Johnny got up and was quicker this time, pushing the stronger cat back.

Licorice immediately got up to help Johnny, but Tiger and Toger stood in his way. Then Tag stood up.

"We don't want any trouble," Tag said, trying to reason with the bullies.

Tiger responded by shoving him in the chest. Tag and Licorice then pushed back Tiger and Toger.

Tag, Licorice, and Johnny did not even realize that the music had stopped and other cats from the alley were starting to gather around. Just as the six cats almost began fighting, though, the five cats in charge of the place rushed in and stopped them. Four of them held back Licorice, Johnny, Toger, and Tugger, while the head cat got in between all of them.

Finally, Toger and Tugger shoved aside the cats holding them. The three bullies huffily left the alley.

Now that everything had calmed down, the five cats in charge and everyone else went back to their business. The music started to play again, and everything returned to normal.

"Are you guys okay?" asked Mary.

"We're fine," said Tag, sounding a bit flustered as he took his seat again.

"They're just jealous because you're the 'rich cats'," April tried to console him.

"Maybe," Tag replied distantly.

"A lot of cats like you guys," Mandy assured them as Mary and April nodded in agreement.

"Well, I guess Tiger, Toger, and Tugger don't like us too well," noted Licorice.

"Well, that's too bad for them," Johnny mumbled under his breath.

The cats' date continued without any further interruptions. Tag, Licorice, and Johnny told their dates about how they had come to live in Suburb City. Tag and Licorice talked about their old home with their parents and the Wistingsly family, and Johnny talked about how he used to sneak out of the house because of his mean owner. He also told the story of how the three cats had been playing in the man's room and had almost gotten caught. The three cats explained how they had been captured and taken to the pet shop and how a woman had almost bought Tag as food for her pet snake. They recounted how the old lady had bought Johnny and then later bought Tag and Licorice, and they explained how they had ended up staying in Suburb City even though they had planned to leave. Then they told the story of how the boss's men had captured Tag and Johnny and how Softy had helped reunite them. Finally, they explained how they had become the rich cats.

Mandy, Mary, and April told Tag, Licorice, and Johnny how they had all come to live in Suburb City. Mandy was the oldest of seven siblings. They had all been living with their parents with a poor family, but when the kittens were old enough, the family had sold them. Mandy's parents had also come from Suburb City and warned her to stay away, but that was exactly where she had been taken. Mary's parents did not know what town they had come from. One day, Mary had run away from home after having a quarrel with her parents. She had gotten lost and nearly starved to death, but after one month of wandering, she had eventually arrived in Suburb City. April was an orphan just like Johnny, and she had been an alley cat like Tag and Licorice. She told the others how she used to live near a train station, where she could often find food. One day, she had gone to sleep in a big boxcar. When she woke up, she discovered that it had traveled to Suburb City. All three girl-cats had chosen to stay when they were taken in by a colony of animals who lived in the cellar of a building. They all had equally interesting stories of how the magic of the Animals' Forest seemed to affect their lives. The six cats discovered that they had much in common.

After that day, Tag, Licorice, and Johnny began to spend more and more time with Mandy, Mary, and April. Through the rest of the summer and into the fall, they went on various escapades throughout the city together and spent a lot of time talking. Sometimes only two of them would go out; other times they would go as a group. Tag and Mandy, Licorice and Mary, and Johnny and April got to know each other better and came to care for each other very much. Before long, without even realizing it, they had fallen in love.

VII
Unwelcome Guests

One morning in late November, the three cats were preparing to go out with their girlfriends. It was 11:30 in the morning, and they had to leave in fifteen minutes. In the living room, Tag was busy trying to arrange a bouquet of flowers that he had bought for Mandy. Licorice, who was all set to go, was sitting on the couch, playing a game of checkers with Softy. Johnny was gazing at his reflection in the glass of the china cabinet, busily licking his paw and trying to pat down some out-of-place fur on top of his head.

Suddenly, the doorbell rang.

The four animals all looked up from what they were doing and stared at each other. Ever since the news reporters had stopped coming, it had become quite unusual for people to visit the cats' house. They knew it must be a person, though, because their animal-friends usually came through the backyard rather than ringing the doorbell.

"Who could it be?" said Johnny.

"A salesman?" suggested Licorice.

"I'll get it," said Tag, gently placing the flowers on the floor. He went to the door while the others waited in the living room.

Tag took a deep breath and called out, "Who is it?"

There was no answer, so it had to be a person, who would not have understood him.

The cats had stacked up some boxes at different levels near the door so that they could easily climb up and look out through the peephole. Tag did just that, nimbly springing up to the top. Looking out through the tiny glass lens, though, he saw nothing but an empty porch. Whoever it was must have left, he concluded.

Tag was curious, though, because it would have been difficult for someone to leave so quickly and not be seen. As he hopped back down, he also wondered if someone might have left a phonebook or some junk mail on the porch. The cats preferred to keep the porch nice and tidy to avoid drawing attention to themselves, so he decided to have a look.

Tag opened the door and stood face to face with a hulking, muscular dog. Behind that dog were two more, just as big. Each of the dogs wore a belt with a set of shackles dangling from it and a scabbard holstering a sword. It was obvious where they were from.

"By orders of King Wolf, all cats at this house will come with us," the first dog stated gruffly. "If you refuse, we'll have to take you by force."

Tag was terrified—all in one second, the warnings of his parents had become true. He quickly tried to close the door, but the stronger, lead dog stopped it with his paw and forced it open.

Tag turned and ran. The three dogs barged in and followed him.

In the living room, Licorice, Johnny, and Softy had only a second to contemplate what kind of commotion they were hearing. Then Tag came flying breathlessly into the room.

"It's the Canine Order!" he alerted the others.

The dogs marched in right after him.

Licorice and Softy instinctively jumped off the couch, and Softy took refuge in the bag of rubber balls. Licorice and Johnny looked every which way, unsure of what to do at first.

"The table," said Johnny, thinking quickly.

He and Licorice got on opposite sides of it. Then, just as Tag ran underneath, the two cats pushed it on its side, blocking the

dogs momentarily.

Unfortunately, one of the dogs just started to go around it on one side while the other two came around on the other side. The cats were forced to retreat to the other side of the room.

The dogs followed with their swords drawn, one moving to the left and the other to the right, trapping the three cats in front of the fireplace. Standing on their hind legs, all three dogs showed perfect balance.

"We need something to fight with," said Licorice.

"How about these?" said Johnny as he withdrew three metal pokers—normally used with the fireplace—from their holder. Tag and Licorice each took one from him. One of the dogs swung his sword strongly at Licorice, but Licorice managed to block the attack—he was just as surprised as the dog.

"Watch it!" ordered the lead dog. "The king wants them *alive!*"

Realizing that the dogs weren't supposed to hurt them too badly, Licorice rose up on his hind legs and swung the poker at the dog several times, but the dog blocked him even more easily. The dog swung back at Licorice. Licorice blocked it and attacked again.

"Surrender now," advised the dog in front of Tag. "It's your only chance."

Tag and Johnny looked at each other.

"No way!" Tag refused.

With that, the two remaining dogs lunged at Tag and Johnny. The two cats defended themselves with the pokers and fought back. They moved away from the fireplace.

One dog chased Johnny, swinging at him aggressively with his sword, and each time he missed, something in the room took the punishment. The dog's sword sent the cats' lamp crashing to the ground. Johnny leaped up onto a cabinet that contained stereo equipment. The dog swung and Johnny jumped again—the stereo equipment received a bad gash across the front of it.

Meanwhile, the lead dog was stalking Tag, trying to figure out how to capture the stubborn cats without injuring them. Tag backed up nervously, his mind racing to think of a way to escape from—or defeat—the stronger, better skilled, and better armed dogs.

Licorice's opponent was becoming frustrated. He swung his sword madly, but with each move, Licorice got better at blocking him. He started to attack the dog back, but then the dog knocked Licorice's poker away from him. Immediately the dog pushed Licorice to the floor. The dog took out the chain he was carrying and prepared to lock it around the cat's legs, but Licorice did two somersaults to get some distance from the dog. He picked up his poker as the dog rushed toward him. The dog swung his sword, but Licorice blocked it and twisted the poker in a loop, removing the sword from the dog's grip and flipping it into the air. Licorice skillfully caught the sword, and the dog backed away in astonishment.

At the same time, Tag and the lead dog were battling again. They swung their weapons and blocked each other adeptly, but with each collision, Tag was knocked back a bit. Finally, one strong blow from the dog sent Tag tumbling to the ground, and the dog stood over him triumphantly, ready to take him into custody. Tag was shaken by the fall, but then he spotted the cats' bag of rubber balls next to the couch. As the dog reached for him, Tag summoned all his energy and lurched towards it, regaining some space between himself and the dog. Grabbing one of the balls, he threw it at the dog with as much force as he could muster. The dog tried to block it with his forearm but missed and got hit in the stomach. Tag started to throw the balls as fast and as hard as he could, finding that the impacts on the dog were just enough to slow him down. The dog raised his paw to protect his face and tried to advance as Tag continued to hurl the balls at him. Softy was almost in a panic as the rubber balls that made up his hiding place began to disappear. Then he started trying to help by handing the balls to Tag. With the dog distracted and off balance but almost within arm's reach, Tag grabbed the handles of the bag. Realizing what Tag was about to do, Softy hoisted himself up by the edges and jumped clear. Tag swung the bag, knocking the dog's sword away from him and spilling the remaining rubber balls all across the living room floor. The dog reacted by lunging at Tag with his forepaws, but Tag ducked underneath, ran a few feet, and scooped up the dog's sword. Turning, he sliced the sword back and forth through the air to ward the dog away, and the dog started to back away from him.

Johnny was angry. He was sick and tired of every animal who thought he was stronger trying to push him around. He started attacking the dog wildly, and the two opponents' weapons clanged against each other loudly. Finally Johnny began to force the dog back. He began to swing the poker even faster, and the dog was having trouble keeping up. Suddenly, the dog slipped on a rubber ball and fell flat on his back. Johnny stood over him victoriously.

The dog looked at his two companions, who had also been defeated. He scrambled to his feet and turned to run. The others followed him, and they all fled through the front door where they had entered.

The three cats followed the intruders and watched them leave the premises. Then, after closing and locking the front door, they returned to the living room and sat down to rest amongst the jumble of rubber balls and damaged furniture. They were just as amazed as they were relieved to have been able to stand their ground against the unwelcome guests. They had no idea *why* the dogs had come for them, but there was no question where they were from—Dog Castle. Now they knew Ralph and Daisy had been right about Suburb City after all. They were eager to tell someone what had just occurred.

"We'd better get going," declared Tag. "We're already going to be late."

Softy emerged from underneath the sofa and looked around nervously.

"You're still going out after this?" he asked. "What if there's more dogs like that out there?"

The three cats looked at each other. It was a good point.

"We have to tell someone," said Licorice. "Don't worry. We'll be careful."

The four animals did a quick job of tidying up the room. Then the three cats headed out. After all the commotion, Tag left the flowers behind.

VIII
The Storyteller

The cats hurried quickly but cautiously through the city and arrived at the Cougar Club Coffee Shop about twenty minutes late. They were eager to see their girlfriends and to tell them what had happened.

As they entered the alley, they were greeted by some of the cats they knew, but for some reason, their friends seemed rather downcast and not very talkative. From a distance, other cats watched them silently. The three of them spotted Mandy and April sitting at their favorite table. Oddly, Mary was not with them.

"Where's Mary?" Licorice inquired as soon as they got to the table.

Mandy and April looked at each other with dour expressions on their faces. Licorice could sense that something was wrong.

"Licorice," Mandy said tenderly, "the Canine Order captured Mary."

Licorice was stunned.

"*What?*" he said slowly.

"Earlier this morning," Mandy explained, "we were out walking. Suddenly, these three dogs with swords jumped out from nowhere."

"One of them told us to surrender, but instead we ran," recalled April.

"But they grabbed Mary," said Mandy sorrowfully. "There was nothing we could do."

"Two of them chased after us," added April, "but we managed to outrun them. We were so scared...we were afraid to come back outside after that, but then we decided to come tell you what happened."

The two cats were almost in tears. Tag and Johnny each gave their girlfriend a hug.

Licorice just sat there. He could not believe that Mary had been taken away.

"Three dogs tried to capture us this morning, too," Tag informed the girls, "at our house."

Mandy and April did not seem surprised.

"Are you okay?" asked Mandy. "They must have known where you lived because you're the 'rich cats'."

"We're fine," replied Tag, "but that's amazing that the Canine Order came after all six of us."

"Not just us," Mandy corrected him. "A lot of cats were attacked yesterday and this morning. So far, fourteen cats have been reported missing."

"What does that mean?" asked Johnny.

"It means...," came a voice from behind him, "they're back!"

Johnny and April turned to see an old, shabby-looking, gray cat. He was partially white, with green eyes. In a few places, some fur was missing. The old cat looked like he had been through a lot in his lifetime.

"It was only a matter of time," added the cat.

"What do you mean?" Tag asked the stranger as he approached them.

"Tell me," the old cat said curiously, "what do you know about Dog Castle?"

"Not much," answered Tag. "We just know about the Animals' Forest and how its magic affects everything around it. We know how King Wolf came to power and how all the other animals were in danger from him. Our parents were sent away from the Forest because of the threat from Dog Castle. But we

ended up living here anyways."

"I'm not surprised," said the old cat. "Almost all the younger animals here had parents or grandparents who lived in the Forest. They ended up back here because of the Forest's magic. And because they don't know much about King Wolf or Dog Castle, they've stayed here like you. All the animals in my generation know to get away from here—or at least keep trying. This is the eighth time I've ended up back in this city."

"Then *you* know about Dog Castle," Tag concluded.

"Oh, yes," answered the old cat. "I used to live in the Forest before the Canine Order attacked. But do you know *why* they attacked?"

By now, some other cats from nearby were approaching to hear the old cat's story.

"To take over the animals' kingdom," Johnny answered.

"That's only part of the reason," stated the cat. "You see, before King Wolf came to power, everything was fine. For many years, all the animals had lived in the Forest in peace. Then one day this cat went exploring in one of the Forest's caves, and he found this crystal. Well, immediately he knew he had made a great discovery. The crystal seemed to have a very high concentration of the magic of the Animals' Forest. The cat said he could sense it, and that it had attracted him to it before he even realized it. He brought it back to the kingdom, and all the animals were able to enjoy its benefits. With the crystal close by, the abilities granted to them by being in the Forest were improved more than ever before. But there was one aspect of the crystal that went beyond anything the animals had ever experienced; sometimes when an animal would touch it, he or she would get a glimpse of the future."

"The future?" repeated Mandy. Many of the cats, including Tag, Licorice, Johnny, Mandy, and April, had heard of the crystal in passing, but they had never thought much about it. Like the animals' old kingdom, it was something that was never talked about much.

"Not what would happen for certain," specified the cat, "but the animals would see a vision of something they might later do—an *idea*...I guess that part of what enables us to create things and have new inventions is the ability to imagine them. Well, when the animals would touch the crystal, what they saw might not even make sense to them at the time, but later on it would become clear and be very helpful. Some animals studied the crystal and became adept at deciphering some of its visions. The council of animals that governed the kingdom began to use the crystal as an effective tool for making decisions, and for over a year the animals' society flourished."

Some of the cats in the crowd began to talk excitedly about the crystal's remarkable qualities, but they hushed as the old cat went on with the story.

"Now, Wolf was a member of the council of animals, and he had always been very ambitious. Often it seemed that all he really cared about was his own power and status, but there were many dogs who supported him. Like the other council members, Wolf used the crystal to make plans for the kingdom, but he became obsessed with it, using it more and more and spending a great deal of time with it. He was able to come up with several good ideas, but he became arrogant, thinking he was stronger and smarter than everyone else and that he knew better than anybody else how to run the kingdom. He ran for head of the animal council, but he was soundly defeated in the election. The next time there was an election, he lost his position entirely.

"But that was when Wolf became dangerous. He gathered a group of dogs and tried to steal the crystal, but he was unsuccessful. The animals tried to arrest him, but he and his group escaped and left the kingdom. Wolf swore revenge that day, and that one day he would rule over all the animals. He wasn't heard from for a while, but it wasn't long before the animals learned that he was recruiting other dogs and constructing a palace of his own called Dog Castle.

"After that, the animals realized that the crystal was a temptation to anyone who wanted its power for themself. The cat who had found the crystal took it into the Forest and hid it. He didn't tell anyone where it was. After a number of years, King Wolf sent a message to the animals' kingdom, demanding that they surrender, be under his rule, and turn over the crystal to him, or he would destroy their kingdom. What the animals didn't know until then was that Dog Castle was actually a fortress, and King Wolf had been using it to secretly train an army. He called his new army of dogs the Canine Order.

"Even though the animals had little time to prepare, they refused his demands, and eventually the Canine Order attacked. The animals briefly tried to fight back, but they didn't have weapons or training like the Canine Order. Some of them didn't survive...but rather than surrendering and becoming King Wolf's subjects, most of the animals abandoned the kingdom and fled. The Canine Order drove the animals out of the Forest, but they were never able to find the crystal."

The crowd was abuzz with quiet conversation. It was obvious that the cats were a little overwhelmed by all they had just heard.

"So why would the Canine Order be back now, kidnapping cats from the city?" questioned Mandy.

"The Order has been searching for the crystal ever since," answered the old, gray cat. "They've sent scouts into the city before, to see what information they could get, and they must have finally realized that the descendants of those from the Animals' Forest keep coming to this city. The crystal has a high concentration of the same power as the Animals' Forest, except it only ever attracted *one* animal to it—the cat who found it. King Wolf has been searching for *that* cat ever since he hid the crystal— but now he must have realized that if the crystal is the same as the Animals' Forest, that cat's descendants may *also* be attracted to it."

"So you mean they're going to make the cats help them look for the crystal," deduced Tag.

"And hope one of them is related to the cat who hid it," added Mandy.

"That's right," answered the storytelling, old cat.

"But what good would the crystal do them now?" questioned April. "There's no one else left in the Forest for him to rule over."

The old cat sighed deeply. He seemed reluctant to answer.

"I'm sure you all know," he began, "how animals in the Forest have even greater abilities than they do here. Right now, the Canine Order can come into the city briefly, keep most of their skills, and try to kidnap us; but if they stay here, after a while, their abilities wear off. If King Wolf can find the crystal, he can take it anywhere he wants, and he and his army will be able to keep all their same abilities wherever they go. Meanwhile, any people would be repelled away from the crystal. The Canine Order could invade any place it wants to…including this city."

With that, the crowd of cats became much more agitated and talkative. Everyone seemed quite anxious.

Tag and Johnny exchanged glances, realizing now why the dogs that morning had been able to stand up and handle their swords so well. It was no less than miraculous that they'd been able to avoid being captured by them.

"Maybe we should go into the Forest and find the crystal for ourselves," suggested one of the cats in the crowd, "before King Wolf finds it."

"The Forest is a big place," responded the old cat, "and it's not safe. You'd be more likely to be caught by the Canine Order than to find the crystal."

"But what if King Wolf finds it?" said another. "Then we'll all be in danger!"

"The crystal was hidden very well. The best thing you can do is to avoid being captured by King Wolf's soldiers."

"What happened to the cat who hid the crystal?" asked another cat.

"He's around somewhere," answered the old cat. "He could even be back in this city again."

Then Licorice, who had been rather quiet, spoke up. "How do you get to Dog Castle?"

The cats in the crowd were silent. They seemed taken aback by the question.

The old cat eyed him sternly. "The castle is located deep within the Animals' Forest," he replied fretfully. "There are many signs on the Forest's trails that point to it—unless the Canine Order removed them." Then the cat's tone turned grave as he spoke to the crowd of cats. "But if any of you are thinking of going there to *rescue* the captured cats, think again. King Wolf's army is very strong, and the castle is invulnerable. There's no way any animal could escape from there. I'm afraid whoever the Canine Order has kidnapped is gone for good."

Licorice couldn't accept that. "But we've got to save them!" he insisted.

"It's too dangerous," the old cat told him. "I know you want to do something, but if you go there, the Canine Order will just capture you, too."

With that, the other cats in the crowd began to bombard the old cat with questions. Mandy and April tried to console Licorice.

"We're sorry, Licorice," said April. "We feel bad, too."

"I know," Licorice replied sadly.

That night, a couple hours after Tag and Johnny had gone to sleep, Licorice sneaked through the hallway and into the living room where they had fought the three dogs earlier that day. He felt very tired; that skirmish already seemed like a distant memory. He quickly checked to see if anyone was around and then picked up one of the two swords that had been left behind. He had spent the last two hours fashioning a harness for the sword out of some cloth and some leather. Now he placed the weapon in the crudely constructed holder and slung it over his shoulder and onto his back. He tightened the strap and walked around in a circle until he was sure the sword would stay on. Then he silently crept to the back door and slipped outside. Unknown to him, Softy had observed him from the bag of rubber balls.

All was calm this cool, autumn evening. The only sound on the night air was the unmindful chirping of a plethora of crickets off in the distance.

Licorice was heading for Dog Castle. He had been thinking about it all day, and he just couldn't let Mary go that easily.

As Licorice tramped across the backyard's thick grass, he recalled when Tag and Johnny had been held captive by the boss more than half a year ago. He had been determined to free them, and in the end, Softy had been successful in helping them—but only after it looked for a while like he wasn't going to make it back. Licorice had considered asking Tag and Johnny to help him, but this time he wasn't willing to put anyone else at risk— especially considering just how risky it was. Furthermore, he knew that if he told them, they would never approve of him going.

Licorice had not yet reached the edge of the cats' extensive property when he thought he heard a door open. He quickened his pace, but before he had even gone ten more feet, he heard his name called.

It was Tag and Johnny. Licorice began to run, but with the sword on his back, he could not move as quickly as them. Before he knew it, they had caught up with him.

"What are you doing out here?" questioned Tag. "Why do you have one of the swords?"

Licorice was still puffing and panting from the sprint. He answered with "Going…to…Dog Castle…"

"Licorice, you're crazy!" exclaimed Tag. "You'll get killed if you go there."

"I've got to save Mary!" Licorice replied hotly.

"All by yourself?" questioned Johnny.

"No one else should have to go," said Licorice. "But if I want to go…I should go."

"You shouldn't go either," replied Tag. "You'll get caught. You heard what that old cat said."

Licorice wasn't sure what to say. "How come? I know how to sword fight. Look how we beat those dogs who tried to capture us."

"You'd be outnumbered!" said Tag with anger and frustration.

"So…? I'll *sneak* in."

For a brief moment, the cats just stared at each other. Licorice could tell he was losing the argument with Tag. He hadn't truly considered *how* he would save Mary.

At the same time, though, the idea made some sense to Johnny. They *had* beaten those three dogs, and if they were sneaky instead of trying to fight their way in, maybe it could be possible. "Maybe we should all go," he suggested.

"No!" Tag snapped, dismayed to have suddenly lost Johnny's support. "Three cats instead of one would still be outnumbered."

"Yeah, I guess you're right," Johnny conceded.

Tag knew he had to convince them. He remembered all too well how it felt when, as kittens, the three of them had been captured by the animal catcher. Because of their intelligence and physical abilities, they had thought that they were so smart and that nothing could happen to them—then they had been taken away from their parents.

"Licorice," he said evenly, "we know you miss Mary, but it's too dangerous."

"But I have to try," Licorice protested. "I can't just do *nothing.*"

"Licorice, you're not going," Tag told him. "And that's final…Sometimes there's just nothing you can do."

"But there has to be…," Licorice replied desperately. He felt extremely tired—it was almost impossible to think.

"Why don't you get some sleep, Licorice," suggested Johnny. "You'll feel better if you can stop thinking about it for a while."

Licorice knew there was no way they were going to let him go, and he didn't want them to drag him all the way back inside. He was just too tired right now to put up the struggle. Grudgingly he accompanied his brother and his friend back to the house. It had been a long day.

IX
Cat Confrontation

In the following days, fewer encounters with King Wolf's dogs were reported. After the initial shock caused by the Canine Order's sudden emergence in Suburb City, some cats had fled the town in an attempt to avoid the danger for at least a little while—before the magic of the Animals' Forest might cause them to return. Those who chose to stay did so either because they felt that running away was useless or because they were unwilling to be frightened away from their homes and their friends. Tag, Licorice, Johnny, Mandy, and April, for both of those reasons, had all decided to stay.

Among those who had chosen to remain in the city, most had adopted good strategies to keep themselves safe. Cats went out together only in large groups. Some went out only when absolutely necessary, such as to obtain food. A few cats had taken on the responsibility of patrolling the city and spreading the word whenever a party of sword-bearing dogs was sighted. Many of the city's dogs and other animals also gave assistance to help alert the cats in case of any danger. Although the need for caution remained, a sense of confidence began to grow amongst the cats of the city.

After one week, a dancing contest was to be held at the Cougar Club Coffee Shop for any animals who wanted to participate. Although everyone was still sad because of the kidnapped cats, most agreed that the contest should still be held. For the cats, going on with the contest was a way of going on with their lives and not letting anyone scare them.

On the morning of the contest, Licorice slept very late. No one had mentioned his attempt to go to Dog Castle since that night, but everyone knew he was still quite sad. In fact, he had done nothing but stay home all week, even when Tag, Johnny, and his other friends had tried to get him to do things. When they all met for breakfast, Tag, Johnny, and Softy tried the difficult task of convincing Licorice to join in the dancing contest. They had discussed the idea during the week with Mandy and April, and they had all agreed that it would be a good way to at least get him out of the house.

Reluctantly, Licorice agreed to go with them. He wasn't particularly excited about the contest, but they had been nagging him all week and he had to admit that maybe they were right…maybe he should just accept that Mary was gone and try to go on with his life.

Later that day, the three cats headed for the Coffee Shop. Softy, as usual, stayed behind. Although Tag, Licorice, and Johnny were his best friends, he knew there were some cats who would sooner consider him a tasty snack than a friend.

The three cats met Mandy and April right on time at their usual table. With them was another cat named Ginger, a friend of April who had volunteered to be Licorice's partner.

"Guess what?" said Mandy. "Your old friends Tiger, Toger, and Tugger are in this contest."

The three cats looked across the alley and saw the bullies sitting at another table.

"I heard they've been *practicing*," April added with a giggle.

"No problem," Johnny told her confidently. "We can beat them."

After they had conversed for a few minutes, the head cat's voice was heard. "May I have your attention please? We're ready to begin the contest. When your name is called, please come up and give your performance! Does everyone understand?"

An array of shouting came from the audience.

"Good luck!" said the cat.

The first pair of cats was called to the stage, and the piano player, Lenny, started to play some of his best music. The two cats performed as best they could, twirling each other every which way and trying to show good timing with the music. After they were finished, all the cats clapped and cheered for them. A panel of judges called out their scores, and another cat called out the average.

Tiger, Toger, Tugger, and their girlfriends each gave their performance. To everyone's surprise, Tugger and his girlfriend were quite good and scored ninety-four percent.

Later on, Licorice and Ginger were called up. Licorice didn't feel much like dancing, though. It felt strange to be dancing with someone other than Mary, and as the music played, he just couldn't concentrate. Several times he moved in a different direction from Ginger, and once he even tripped. When they finished, they received a score of only sixty-five percent. Licorice apologized to Ginger, but she understood.

The next group was Tag and Mandy, but they also failed to beat Tugger and his girlfriend, scoring only eighty-one percent. After seeing how Licorice and Ginger had performed, it was hard for them to do their best either.

The last group was Johnny and April. They had seen how difficult it had been for Licorice and Ginger, as well as for Tag and Mandy. Before going on stage, they determined to set their emotions aside, just for the time being, and really concentrate on what they were doing.

The two of them were able to pull off a great performance, and all the cats cheered loudly when they finished. Everyone hoped they would beat Tugger, but as the scores were announced, the average amounted to only ninety-one percent.

After that, awards were presented to the winners. The head cat announced the third place winners, who happened to be the first group that had performed. The two partners accepted purple ribbons with small ornaments at the end that represented bronze medals.

Second place was awarded to Johnny and April. A smattering of applause and whistling rippled through the audience as they were presented with a pair of silver medals. While the two of them were pleased with their performance, they were a bit disappointed that they had been unable to win the contest.

First place was awarded to Tugger and his girlfriend, who each received a gold medal. While Tiger, Toger, and their girlfriends yelled wildly in approval, a few cats in the crowd booed and hissed. Tugger smugly strutted around on the stage, holding the medal above his head.

Tag, Licorice, Johnny, Mandy, April, and Ginger could only watch as Tugger showed off. They wished that at least one of their groups might have beaten him.

A few minutes after the awards ceremony, the six cats sat at their table, discussing how the contest had gone. Suddenly, though, they noticed Tiger, Toger, and Tugger approaching. Licorice, especially, started feeling on edge. He tried to avoid making eye contact with the bullies. Tugger spoke mostly to Johnny at first, however.

"Nice dancing, rich cat," the sore winner commented in a condescending, sarcastic tone. "Too bad being rich didn't help you dance any better." Tiger and Toger chuckled derisively along with him.

Johnny didn't care who had won. He knew he and April had done a fine job, especially under the circumstances. "Yeah," he replied. "That is too bad."

"Maybe if you were *more* famous, you could have won."

"Maybe," Johnny replied coolly. After their confrontation with the three soldier-dogs a week ago, these bullies no longer seemed so bothersome to him.

"But he was the good one," Tiger jumped in, since they weren't getting much reaction from Johnny. "How about Tag? He was terrible!"

The others started laughing.

Tag looked at his friends. He knew if he said anything, he would be asking for trouble. Besides, it wasn't worth a confrontation on account of something so trivial.

Meanwhile, the three bullies were laughing like crazy, insulting Tag and Mandy's performance and mimicking their moves.

Then Toger noticed Licorice staring down at the table. "And how about Licorice?" he said. "He was even worse."

Licorice bristled as he heard his name mentioned and the three cats cackling even more rowdily.

"He got the worst score of anyone," Tiger pointed out.

"Yeah, that's right!" Toger remembered.

Licorice looked up angrily. He knew the three cats were well aware of why he had performed poorly.

"Aw, what's the matter?" taunted Toger. "*Someone* had to be the worst."

Licorice felt enraged. If they mentioned Mary…

"He must miss his old girlfriend," Toger went on callously. "Too bad the Order got 'er." The three bullies were laughing very loudly now.

Licorice couldn't stand it anymore. He furiously leaped up from his seat and threw himself at the larger cat, tackling him. The two of them started rolling around on the ground, trying to pin each other down. Tag and Johnny knew they had to stop them, but when they got up, Tiger and Tugger pushed each of them aside. Soon they were pushing and shoving each other as well.

It was not long before the head cat, the piano player, and the other helpers came to stop the fighting. They first managed to restrain Tag, Johnny, Tiger, and Tugger, but Licorice was the hardest one to stop. Even after one of the waiters had grabbed him, he continued to fight and kick, trying to get away. Being seized by the waiter only frustrated him more.

"Stop it, Licorice!" yelled Tag.

"He's crazy!" hollered Toger. "Did you see how he attacked me?"

Eventually Licorice settled down. The head cat told Tag, Johnny, and the girls that Licorice would have to leave. They all left the alley with him.

When they got home, Tag, Licorice, and Johnny discussed the confrontation, and Licorice acknowledged that he shouldn't have let Toger get to him. By starting to fight, he knew he had escalated the situation unnecessarily.

Tag and Johnny knew that Licorice still felt bad about Mary, so they all agreed to forget about the incident. However, now Licorice felt more determined than ever to go to Dog Castle.

X
Off into the Night

That night, Licorice crept down the hall and opened the door to the closet, where the cats had decided to store the two swords. Quietly he retrieved one of the swords and placed it in the leather contraption he had devised to carry it.

Licorice slinked out into the cold night, this time without being detected. He was on his way to Dog Castle.

Licorice made his way through town, treading down streets he had never visited before. He had just enough familiarity with the city to have a general idea of which way to go. Before long, he had left his wealthy neighborhood behind and was meandering through a more quaint part of the city. Gradually, the area became more rustic in appearance, with more trees, plants, and patches of dirt and weeds surrounding a decreasing number of cabin-style homes. Within a few hours, he reached the edge of town, where the community gave way to a dense forest. Licorice knew it was the Animals' Forest, and there would be no more human-made structures past this point. Without hesitation, he marched ahead.

As soon as Licorice entered the Forest, he could feel that something was different. He could tell that he now had greater abilities than he had possessed in the city. His thoughts seemed somehow clearer, and he had a feeling of greater physical strength and dexterity. His senses seemed heightened, too, but perhaps that was just due to being in a new place. He also had a familiar sense of belonging in the Forest, even though he had never been there before. He knew it must be the Forest attracting him there, as his parents had once described. Even if it was, he decided, he didn't care; he still had to save Mary. He started walking on his hind legs, which felt perfectly natural now.

As Licorice ventured further into the Forest's dark interior, he noticed that the vegetation was rich and wild. An owl hooted and a cold breeze swept by, sending a shiver down his spine. A sudden rustling in the bushes nearby caused him to turn with a start. A harmless groundhog scuttled by and looked out at him from the base of a large fern.

Licorice's mind began to play tricks on him. Snarled-up, foreboding trees seemed to jump out at him. Twisted roots looked like bizarre creatures.

Suddenly, Licorice tripped and hit the cold, damp ground. The impact was jarring, but nothing was injured other than his pride. As he got up and shook the mud from his forepaws, he figured it must have rained recently. Low, thick clouds filled the sky and nearly obscured the moon. He swatted at a mosquito that buzzed by. Sounds of frogs, crickets, and crows unsettled him as he moved on.

After a while, a thick fog rolled in, making visibility poor. Licorice moved on though, determined to find Dog Castle. He soon happened upon what seemed like a narrow trail, and he decided to follow it.

It began to rain. Licorice trudged determinedly through the mud in the heavy fog. A flash of lightning lit up the sky not far away and within half a second the shockwave of the thunder came crashing over him. The sudden impact and sheer power of the thunder were both awesome and startling. He continued uneasily.

Eventually the rain stopped, and the forest became calm once again. A delicate cascade of water droplets continued to trickle from the forest canopy above. At some point Licorice began to notice a strange rustling sound which would come and go, emanating sometimes from his right and sometimes from his left

but always from behind him. He decided it must be his imagination again. At last he saw a signpost up ahead and a fork in the path. He hurried over to them.

There were two arrows on the sign. One pointed to the left and read "The Kingdom." The other pointed to the right and read "Beware: Dog Castle." Licorice took a nervous but determined deep breath. Though the animals' old kingdom was a far more inviting destination, he stayed on course for Dog Castle.

Licorice had been walking for a while longer when he noticed something large coming into view ahead. He looked up and saw, partially obscured by dark branches and leaves, not far away, Dog Castle!

Dog Castle was an awesome monstrosity built erect with several stories. It might have been Licorice's imagination, but the fortress seemed to have the face of a dog, and the face seemed to be staring ominously at him. A portcullis in the shape of fangs flanked a tongue-like drawbridge. Windows formed the eyes and nose. A moat encircling the exterior took the form of a spiky collar.

The drawbridge was partially raised, but at this time of night, Licorice wasn't surprised. He had known all along that he would have to find a creative way of getting inside. For lack of a better idea, he left the path and headed in a slightly different direction so he could approach the castle from the side. As he drew nearer, he was able to distinguish the figures of at least two lookouts on patrol behind the upper wall of the castle.

Licorice's senses were extremely heightened now. He heard the same peculiar rustling again and stopped briefly to investigate the bushes off to his left. He thought he saw something large and furry darting away, but it was gone in an instant.

There was nothing to do but continue. Staying hidden amongst the thick forest foliage, Licorice succeeded in sneaking up very close to the huge fortress. Then, while the nearest lookout had strolled out of sight, he cautiously emerged from the bushes and approached the edge of the castle's moat for a closer look. Four alligators in the moat surfaced and drew dangerously near, and Licorice readied his sword. Abruptly, one of the gators raised its snout out of the water.

"Going for a swim, kitty cat?" it hissed sarcastically.

Licorice stumbled backwards in fright, but the gators were not bothering to come out of the water. He lowered his sword, realizing he wouldn't need it just yet.

For the moment, Licorice was stymied. Though he was quite close to the castle, there was no obvious way to get in or even to cross the moat. Looking up, he could see that there were several windows above.

Then he had an idea. A giant tree nearby had several branches that reached across the moat and touched the side of the castle. He could remember climbing the tree in Johnny's backyard when he was younger. Though this tree was much taller, he suspected that the magic of the Forest would enable him to climb it. He would crawl out on one of the branches and enter through one of the windows.

As one of the lookouts wandered back into view, Licorice alertly darted back into the cover of the bushes. He glanced back up at the castle wall and checked to make sure he had not been noticed. Then he looked up into the large tree and prepared to start climbing. Suddenly, though, he heard a twig snap, and a spine-chilling sensation came over him; there was someone close by— very close. He was afraid to move, but he whirled around quickly, with his sword raised.

What he saw was not a dog though—or a cat. It was a rabbit.

"Shhhhh!" said the rabbit, holding up one paw in front of his fuzzy, whiskered muzzle. "What are you doing here?"

The rabbit did not seem very afraid of Licorice, in spite of the sword he was brandishing. He was mostly beige with several patches of white, and his long, floppy ears drooped down almost in front of his eyes. He was rather large for a rabbit, and Licorice guessed that the Forest's magic had something to do with it. Now he knew his senses had not been deceiving him.

"Why have you been following me?" Licorice asked.

"Not many cats wandering the Animals' Forest these days..." the rabbit answered knowingly. "I just wanted to warn you—go back now while you have the chance."

Licorice had not come this far only to be stopped by a rabbit he didn't even know. "I can't do that," he replied curtly. Since the rabbit didn't seem to be a threat, he turned and again prepared to climb the tree.

"I know why you're here," said the rabbit.

Licorice was almost shocked. How could the rabbit know about Mary?

"You're here to rescue the cats that were captured," the rabbit said.

Licorice nodded as he realized—the rabbit knew nothing about him specifically or his girlfriend, but much about the Canine Order and its activities. He turned back curiously, wishful for some help but unsure if it would be wise to reveal his intentions.

"And if I am?"

"Don't do it," the rabbit urged him. "You'll be caught for sure."

Licorice was becoming annoyed. First, everyone else had tried to talk him out of it, now this.

"I have to try," he said softly. Then, feeling that there was nothing else to be gained from the conversation, he turned back toward the tree, placed his rear paw on a notch in the bark, and prepared to hoist himself up.

The rabbit seemed distraught that Licorice wasn't listening to him. He paced back and forth anxiously.

"Then at least…at least let me give you some advice," insisted the rabbit.

Keeping his back to the rabbit this time, Licorice paused to listen. It wouldn't hurt to hear the suggestion.

"Enter through the third window up, second from the right. That's my friend's room. His name is Guarddog. Tell him Harie sent you. You can trust him. Maybe he can help you."

Licorice looked up and located the window Harie had indicated. It was reachable by one of the tree branches.

"Thanks," he said, giving the rabbit a brief, grateful nod. There was no way to know for sure if the advice was reliable, but one window was as good as another. *Any* window was probably just as dangerous.

Licorice began climbing the tree. As soon as he got as high as he wanted, he looked back down. The rabbit was nowhere in sight, but the gators were still lurking in the water below. He hoped he remembered the right window.

As Licorice crawled his way forward on the branch, the thinner and weaker it became. As he neared the window, it almost felt as if it would collapse. The end was bent down below the window, but Licorice was only a few feet away now. He took a deep breath; it was time to go in.

Licorice bent his knees and then hopped softly onto the window ledge. In the dark room, there was just enough moonlight for him to recognize the figure of a medium-sized dog, who seemed to be asleep on a dog-sized bed. Although Harie had said the dog would help him, Licorice felt inclined to just sneak by quietly, if that was possible. As he let himself down from the ledge, though, his sword slid out from its holder, clanged against the windowsill, and noisily dropped to the floor.

As Licorice fumbled in the dark clumsily for his sword, the startled dog whispered, "Who goes there?"

Licorice instinctively raised the sword up off the floor, but the dog showed no aggressive intentions.

"Don't be afraid," he whispered to Licorice, sitting up on the bed and holding out his empty front paws. "I won't hurt you. Who are you? You can trust me."

Somehow, Licorice felt he could trust the dog. After all, the dog hadn't attacked him yet.

"My name is Licorice. Harie told me I should find you. I'm here to rescue the kidnapped cats."

"I'm Guarddog," the dog replied, "and it's a good thing Harie sent you here, or you'd have already been caught. Now listen carefully; you've got to get out of here. Even if I helped you, there's no way you could get all the way down to the dungeon *and* get back out."

"I can't do that," Licorice explained, this time to the dog. "I haven't come all this way just to go back."

The dog did not respond at first, so Licorice headed toward the door.

"Wait!" said the dog. "I don't want to see any more cats get captured."

Licorice turned. "Why do you care about me?" he asked.

The dog sighed. "I don't want King Wolf to get the crystal, and I don't think it was right for him to try to steal it in the first place...You know about the crystal, right?"

"Yes," Licorice answered surely, even though he had only heard the complete story a week ago.

"Well, the king believes that the cat who hid the crystal *or* one of his descendants will be attracted to it, like the way animals are attracted to this forest. The more cats he captures, the more chance he has that one of them will be the one he's looking for— and the more chance he'll have of finding it. For all we know, *you* could be that cat."

"*Me?*" said Licorice with surprise.

"It could be anyone," the dog told him. "The effects of the Forest—and the crystal—are very powerful, and they can cause animals to make decisions that will lead them back to it. If you leave now, we won't have to find out."

Licorice was beginning to feel some doubts about his objective. He had no knowledge of any relation to the cat who had hidden the crystal, but it *would* be quite difficult to save the captured cats. Why hadn't he realized it before? Maybe the Forest or even the crystal had affected his judgment after all. Maybe he *should* leave now, while he still had the chance. Through the window, he could see that the sky had grown distinctly bluer, indicating that dawn was fast approaching. Whatever he was going to do, he knew he'd better do it soon, before all the dogs woke up.

"Then why are you here?" he questioned the dog, while at the same time trying to make up his mind. "If you don't support King Wolf, why are you in this army? Why don't you just leave?"

"Because," answered Guarddog, "this is my home. This place is all I know...I wouldn't know what to do if I left here."

"Well, there's a million things you could do if you left here," Licorice said with a curious frown.

"It's not just that," Guarddog responded. "I mean, I wouldn't know *how* to live anywhere else. I've lived here all my life, and I've come to depend on this place for everything, even shelter and food. It's funny...I'm one of King Wolf's best fighters...I've learned to fight and handle a sword and a spear here and I'm not afraid of anything—except leaving here."

Licorice was surprised to hear the dog admit that he was scared. "My friends and I used to depend on our owner to provide everything for us," he told him. "But after she died, we learned to take care of ourselves. You could do it, too."

"Maybe," Guarddog replied. "But the other thing is that there's the risk of getting caught. King Wolf will hunt down and execute anyone who tries to desert. If it were easy to travel far from here, that would be one thing, but as you know, the Forest has a way of bringing animals back to it. So what's the use?"

"Do all the dogs here feel the same way as you?" Licorice inquired.

"There are many dogs who want to be here, including some of the ones born here, who believe what King Wolf has told them about how glorious it will be when they find the crystal. On the other hand, after the invasion of the animals' kingdom and the crystal wasn't obtained, some dogs did leave, and many others wanted to. That was when King Wolf turned to fear and intimidation as a way of keeping dogs in this dreadful army. Many dogs *would* probably leave, but they fear the consequences of getting caught; plus they just wouldn't know how to live anyplace else. Instead, they've done like me—accepted this place as their home. I may not support King Wolf, but at least I can get food here, I have a nice place to sleep, and I can live in the Forest."

"But what if the king's plan is successful? What if he finds the crystal?"

Guarddog paused at first, unsure of what to say. "I don't know," he finally admitted.

Licorice felt aggravated. These dogs were doing everything King Wolf said—including kidnapping his girlfriend—and some of them didn't even really want to be there. "At least I want to do *something*," he muttered, even though he sincerely doubted his plan now.

Guarddog did not take his statement kindly. "I helped Harie escape from here, when he was a prisoner," he informed the troublesome cat. "That's why he thought maybe I could help you. When there's something I can do, I do it. But in this case, there's just too many guards. I would help you free the cats downstairs, but there's no sense in us *both* getting caught."

Just then, the door to the room was slammed open. Five dogs stood at the entrance.

"Don't move!" ordered the one in front.

Guarddog was taken by surprise and suddenly became very nervous. "General Doverman…"

The other four dogs stormed in with their swords raised. Licorice readied his weapon, and Guarddog pulled a large sword out from under the bed. The four dogs stopped in front of them, ready for battle, as several more appeared, barring the doorway. Licorice and Guarddog knew they were heavily outnumbered.

"The lookouts spotted a cat climbing in here," the general explained to Guarddog, who had not yet raised his sword in any particular direction.

Guarddog's eyes opened wide as he realized that the general did not know he had been friendly to Licorice. Licorice realized it as well.

"He surprised me while I was asleep," Guarddog told the general as he then held the sword toward Licorice. "He's crazy!"

With that, Licorice tried to make a break for it. He headed for the open window, but just as he climbed up, two dogs grabbed him by the shoulders and roughly yanked him down to the floor.

"You had better surrender!" General Doverman warned him.

"It's no use," Guarddog advised him. "There's nothing you can do." By now there were at least ten dogs in the room with them.

Lying flat on his back, Licorice felt the impulse to resist, but with four dogs standing over him, he knew Guarddog was right. He knew the dog was trying to protect him.

Licorice was escorted out of the room under heavy security, and Guarddog voluntarily went along with the group. In talking to the other dogs, Guarddog made it sound as though he were angry at Licorice for coming into his room, but Licorice could tell that the dog was actually trying to look out for him.

The corridors of Dog Castle were composed of dreary, gray stone and lit by wall-mounted candles. In the light, Licorice noticed that Guarddog was light brown. A portion of his face was white, as was his belly. He had sensitive, light brown eyes like a puppy, but his face revealed an expression of cool, confident awareness. He was probably a couple of years older than Licorice. General Doverman was a tall, black dog with stern, golden eyes and a commanding presence.

The group's first stop was in a room downstairs that served as the dogs' blacksmith station. Stored throughout the room were numerous supplies, including various tools and objects constructed out of iron. In the center of the room was an anvil, and lying nearby were a pair of tongs and a hammer. In the back of the room was a forge with a fire that was just beginning to smolder. The smell of the smoke filled Licorice with a sense of dread.

The blacksmith dog measured the length and width of Licorice's hind legs and then proceeded to rummage through his supplies. He soon found a chain with locking shackles at each end and snapped it on each of Licorice's hind legs. As the dogs led him away from that room, Licorice discovered that the length of the chain was just long enough to let him walk on all fours; it would have been difficult to walk on his hind legs and certainly impossible to run.

As the guards led him through part of the fortress that was open to the sky, Licorice could see that it was light now. Morning had come, and many dogs were already stirring within the castle.

The dogs conducted Licorice down another flight of stairs to the dungeon area, which was enclosed by a wall of iron bars. The main gate was unlocked, and the dogs led him inside. Licorice expected to see a number of imprisoned cats, but instead the dungeon was completely empty.

Within the main dungeon area were four cells, each with its own door. The guards shoved Licorice into the nearest one and slammed the door behind him. The general locked it himself.

"I'm sure the king will want to pay this cat a visit," he said to Guarddog. "We should go report to him."

Guarddog nodded in agreement. They both knew that the king preferred to have a look at every prisoner taken to see if he or she bore a resemblance to the cat who had hidden the crystal. Licorice would surely be no exception. The general ordered a few dogs to remain behind and guard the solitary prisoner.

Guarddog took one last look at Licorice as he accompanied the general out of the dungeon. He felt bad that Licorice had been captured, but he knew there was nothing more he could have done.

Licorice caught the dog's glance and was grateful that at least he hadn't gotten him in trouble. He knew the dog agreed with his intentions, but after all, the dog had been smart not to try to help him.

Alone in the cell, Licorice wondered where the other cats were. Both Harie and Guarddog had mentioned them, but if they weren't in the dungeon, where were they? His thoughts then turned to finding some way to escape, but without the key, he knew it was impossible. He grasped the bars of the cell, realizing they were too close together for any cat to fit through. Hopelessly he sank to the floor and wished he had never come to Dog Castle.

XI
An Army of Animals

Tag, Johnny, and Softy woke up that morning and discovered that Licorice was gone. Usually none of the four animals ever went anywhere without telling the others, and after what had happened the day before, they were all a bit worried. The three of them split up to search the mansion. It took them over thirty minutes to search every room plus the backyard.

When they regrouped in the living room, none of them had found any sign of their friend, but Johnny had discovered a clue to where he might be. Softy noticed that he looked extremely concerned.

"Where do you think he is?" asked the perceptive mouse.

"Well, I just looked in the hall closet...," Johnny said delicately.

Tag looked startled.

"Oh, no...," Softy muttered.

"And only one of the swords was there," Johnny informed them.

Tag shook his head back and forth slowly because he knew what it meant. "He went to Dog Castle."

"We've got to save him!" declared Softy.

They were all quiet for a moment until Tag spoke up. "How can we?" he said glumly. "We'd be outnumbered just the same as him."

"Well, we've got to do something," said Johnny. "First Mary was captured, and now Licorice will be, too…he's your brother and my friend…we can't just sit here!"

"Maybe we can stop him before he gets there," Softy suggested, "if we hurry…"

"I doubt it," Johnny replied solemnly. "He probably left last night."

"Yeah, you're right…," realized Softy.

Tag felt a great conflict inside himself. He remembered very well how it felt when he had been separated from his parents, and now his brother was gone. He wanted to do something, but going off by themselves the same as Licorice had done didn't seem like the best way. If only there was some way to save Licorice, Mary—and all the others—without rashly going off by themselves…

They all sat there in disbelief, each of them grasping for any notion that would make the situation better. For a few minutes no one said anything.

It seemed there was just nothing they could do, so Johnny tried to say something hopeful. "Well," he began, "we don't *know* that he was captured. Maybe he changed his mind and went someplace else—or maybe he went there but then turned back." He didn't really believe it himself.

"Maybe…," Tag replied pensively. "But what if Licorice was *right*?" he said, surprising the others, "—not about going by himself, but just about going. How many cats have been captured already? And what's going to stop King Wolf from capturing more? We can't just leave the city because we know we'll just end up back here. So, where's it going to end? Maybe we need to do *something*…even if Licorice *didn't* get captured."

Johnny agreed with this line of thinking. "Well, when the Canine Order attacked the kingdom, they drove the animals out," he said. "What do we have that those animals didn't?"

"Well, we've fought some of those dogs—at least you and I have—so we know we can stand up to them. Those animals didn't even have any swords. They couldn't even defend themselves."

"If we just had enough animals, including dogs, with swords, we could stand up to the Canine Order," said Johnny.

All of a sudden, Tag's face lit up. "We'll need an *army* of animals!"

"Okay," said Johnny anxiously. "Our first stop'll be Brian's house. He knows this city like the back of his paw. If anyone knows where we can get some swords, it's him. Then we can split up and round up more animals."

"Okay," Tag agreed. "Let's get going."

Softy went along with his two friends. Although he tended to be nervous about meeting other cats, he was determined to help Licorice, who had once saved him from a particularly nasty mousetrap. As long as he stayed with Tag and Johnny, he knew he would be safe.

Their first destination was the house of Johnny's friend, Brian. Johnny reached up and rang the doorbell. Softy stood out of sight in the hedges, since people usually did not react well to seeing mice. A nice lady opened the door.

She said with a smile, "Oh, the 'rich cats.' Just a minute…" She called Brian, who came scampering out the door. He was an orange and white cat with orange eyes, a bit younger than Tag and Johnny. Brian loved exploring, and he was always telling stories about the places he had visited around the city.

"What do you guys wanna do?" he asked gleefully.

Johnny, with a straight face, answered. "Brian, we're here for business."

The smile on Brian's face vanished instantly and matched Johnny's look. Tag's expression was grim as Johnny continued.

"Brian, last night Licorice went off to Dog Castle to try to rescue Mary. We're gathering an army of animals to save them and the others. Will you—" Brian interrupted, but Johnny was glad he didn't have to finish the plea.

"Yeah, I'll help!"

The look on Johnny's face turned to a grin. He looked at Tag, then back at Brian. "You wouldn't happen to know where we can get some swords, would you?"

Brian thought for a moment. "Maybe…maybe…the old scrap yard? I think I've seen some there."

"Are you sure?" asked Tag.

"The old scrap yard," Brian said positively.

"Okay," said Tag. "Softy and I will round up some more animals while you guys go get the swords. We'll meet back at our house."

The two pairs headed off in different directions.

The first animal Tag and Softy encountered was an alley cat, a friend of the rich cats named Ben. Ben had long, dusty-gray fur and orange eyes. Because of his extra-long fur, he looked bigger than the average cat, even though it was only fur. Ben had chosen to live on his own, with neither a person nor other animals, and because he sometimes let his long fur remain messy and dirty, some animals shied away from him and were a bit apprehensive of him. Although Ben was a bit of a loner, Tag, Licorice, and Johnny had found him to be a really good cat underneath it all.

Tag and Ben began to chat while Softy looked around the alley where Ben lived. On one side of the alley were a number of old, dilapidated homes, and on the other side were a chain link fence and an empty field.

Unseen by Tag or Ben were a pair of dogs resting under the stairway of a house's back porch. The dogs' ears perked up when they heard the two cats talking. These two dogs did not have swords, but they happened to be agents of King Wolf, spies who lived in the city.

As the dogs eavesdropped on the conversation, they peered around the stairs and immediately recognized Tag as one of the "rich cats." King Wolf had been eager to capture the rich cats and had been furious when his first attempt failed. The two dogs looked at each other with the same thing in mind—if they could capture Tag, the king would reward them greatly.

"…a whole *army*," Tag was saying to Ben.

"How many animals do you think you can get?" Ben asked.

"Hopefully maybe over one hundred," Tag answered, "— cats *and* dogs."

The dogs heard *that*, too. Quietly they sneaked to a closer position.

Softy saw the dogs and noticed that they were behaving suspiciously. He began to pull on Tag's tail to get his attention. Unfortunately, Tag was too busy talking with Ben.

Suddenly the two dogs began charging across the alley, but the sound of their paws galloping on the pavement gave them away. Tag and Ben looked up with surprise.

At first, Tag did not realize the dogs' intent, but at the last second, he ducked down and dove to his side—one of the dogs' forearms glanced right across the top of his head as they both tried to tackle him. Tag tumbled jarringly on the asphalt, then sprang to his feet, avoided a second effort by one of the dogs, and took off toward the other side of the alley. The two dogs didn't care about Ben at all and went right after Tag.

Tag hurried up the nearest staircase, and the dogs followed closely and noisily behind. Tag reached the top with the dogs right on his tail.

From there, Tag leaped onto the banister and slid down while the dogs lumbered back down the steps. Tag raced back across the alley to the fence at the other side. The two dogs followed him and trapped him there.

"You're coming with us," growled one of the dogs.

"To see King Wolf," the other added giddily.

"I'm not going anywhere," Tag refused.

"We'll see about that," replied the first dog.

Just as the two dogs were about to pounce, Ben was there, grabbing their tails. As the dogs tried to jump, they both fell flat on their stomachs. The two dogs angrily turned to face Ben.

"Stay out of this," the first dog warned. "This is none of your business."

"He's my friend!" Ben replied. "If you want him, you'll have to go through me."

Ben clenched his paws into fists and prepared to fight the heavier and stronger dogs. Tag was surprised to see just how brave Ben was.

"If you insist," threatened the dog.

"Ben!" called Tag, having climbed partway up the fence. Softy had run underneath to the other side.

Ben ran one way down the alley, hoping to go around the dogs and get to the fence. The two dogs followed him to try to stop

him, but suddenly Ben stopped and headed back the other way. He dashed to where Tag was, with the dogs close behind. With a last effort, the furious dogs lunged at him, but he jumped up and Tag pulled him out of their reach. The two dogs crashed right into the fence, causing it to shake violently. The two cats reached the top of the fence, dropped down into the field, and scurried away before the dogs had a chance to follow.

Once they found a place to rest, Tag finished what he was saying to Ben. From the way Ben had stood up to the two dogs,

Tag knew he would be a great help against the Canine Order, even if he *was* a little crazy. Ben agreed to help, and the three of them went to search for more animals to join them.

Meanwhile, the two spy-dogs headed off to Dog Castle to report what they had learned about Tag's plan.

While Tag was busy trying to enlist animals, Johnny and Brian returned to the mansion to get some money to buy the swords. Then they made their way to the scrap yard, which was located on the outskirts of town on the farthest side away from the Animals' Forest. It took them a couple of hours to get there.

The area was surrounded by a chain link fence and gate with loops of sharp, spiky barbed wire on top. Within the scrap yard were numerous mounds of mixed and mashed metal items that were either available for sale or due to be melted down and recycled into something new. There were rows of crushed or otherwise demolished cars, and many waiting to be crushed. There were also old appliances, such as washers, driers, refrigerators, dishwashers, and old computers, and countless stacks of miscellaneous, indiscernible parts. The two cats scanned the whole area until Brian located a bunch of swords atop one of the heaps of assorted metal objects.

"There they are," he said, pointing. "And we can use *that* to transport them," he added, motioning to a shopping cart that had been abandoned nearby on the sidewalk.

Brian led Johnny through a hole in the fence. As the two cats rounded a stack of used tires, they saw two men through the window of a rickety old office trailer. One of the scrap dealers was at work, typing on a computer, while the other was asleep with his feet up on the desk.

"Well, that's them," said Brian reluctantly. "They own this place, I think."

Cautiously, the two cats approached the trailer. Johnny carried several thousand dollars with him in a small pouch.

Suddenly, the man who was typing looked up and noticed them. At first he just looked back down, but then he quickly looked back up again, squinting with disbelief as he noticed the pouch, which was overflowing with money. He abruptly shook the shoulder of his dozing comrade, who nearly fell out of the chair.

The other man looked out the window and immediately realized what his friend was seeing. The two of them looked at each other incredulously, then got up and emerged from the side of the trailer.

"Here, kitty, kitty, kitty...," both men started saying, hunching over and approaching the two cats. Apparently, these two men were *not* accustomed to dealing with Suburb City animals, as other people in the city were.

Johnny emptied about a thousand dollars from the pouch into a small pile on the ground. He pointed to the mound of metal parts that included the swords and began communicating, as he had learned, through meowing and gesturing.

One of the men, with a glimmer of avarice in his eye, immediately snatched up most of the money Johnny had laid out. His friend tried to grab it from him, and the two of them began grappling for the cash. Before long, some of the bills were knocked loose and floated down to the ground. The first man still had most of the cash, while the second began to gather up all the loose bills.

Since the men had taken the money—*much* more than the swords were actually worth—Johnny and Brian went to go get the swords. Unfortunately, the scrap dealers had a different idea. The man who had only been able to garner a few of the bills noticed the cats walking away with the pouch—which contained considerably more.

"Hey! Come back here, you lousy cats!" he shouted angrily. His friend looked up from counting his newfound gain and realized the same thing. Both men started to run toward the two cats.

Johnny and Brian knew that dealing with people was always a little problematic, but they hadn't expected this kind of a response *after* paying for the swords. They sprinted forward several yards until they could duck behind one of the larger scrap piles. The men followed them around the corner.

The two cats started climbing up the mound of metal. The men tried to follow them, but one of them slipped, fell backwards, and hit his head. The two cats glanced back and cringed as they heard the painful-sounding ding of metal against the man's skull.

While that man sat at the edge of the metal pile rubbing the back of his head, the other dealer stopped to see if his buddy was okay. With the two men out of the picture for the time being, Johnny and Brian finally had an opportunity to gather up the swords.

The two cats made several trips back and forth between the pile of swords and the hole in the fence, carrying as many swords at a time as they could. Once they had gathered up all the swords, about twenty-five, and dumped them in the shopping cart, they prepared to get under way. Briefly they looked back through the fence and saw one of the scrap dealers bringing his friend a bag of ice to hold against his head. Then the two men began counting out the money they had acquired and dividing it up evenly. Together, Johnny and Brian began pushing the shopping cart away from the scrap yard. They left in a hurry to meet with Tag.

It took Johnny and Brian a while to wheel the squeaky cart all the way back through town. By nightfall, they wearily approached the mansion. Johnny worried that they probably didn't have enough swords yet, but it had already taken far longer than expected to acquire them. By now, they really needed to get back and regroup with Tag.

"We'll probably need more swords," he advised Brian, so his friend could try to think of another place. As they got closer, though, they saw Tag and some other cats out in front on the sidewalk. As it turned out, the number of swords would be the least of their concerns. Besides Tag, there were only six other cats—and no dogs. Among the group were Mandy and April.

"What are you doing here?" Johnny asked them as he and Brian finally let go of the shopping cart.

"We ran into them at the Cougar Club Coffee Shop," explained Tag.

"Mary and Licorice are our friends, too," stated April. "*We're* coming with you."

"Besides, you're going to need all the help you can get," added Mandy.

Tag and Johnny just nodded understandingly. Although they were worried for their girlfriends' safety, they knew they had a right to come and that they could use their help.

There were only four other cats that Tag had managed to enlist. One was Ben.

There was Richard, a gray cat with black stripes and yellow eyes. Richard had been extremely reluctant to join the army of animals, but somehow Tag and Ben had managed to talk him into it. Although Richard felt that they were *both* crazy, he was a very loyal friend to Tag, Licorice, and Johnny. He had to help his friends.

Blackey and Whitey, the two brothers, were also there. Each of them had orange eyes and medium-length fur, but Blackey was mostly black and Whitey was mostly white. Whitey was very young and very adventurous. He had agreed immediately to join the group because he wanted to be a hero and be famous like "the rich cats." Blackey was the older of the two and had always looked out for his younger brother. When he found out that Whitey had agreed to help their friends, he had no choice but to join as well.

They had a small group: Tag, Johnny, Softy, Mandy, April, Brian, Ben, Richard, Blackey, and Whitey. Although Tag and Johnny were not sure how much help Softy, a small mouse, could be, they understood his desire to help them and Licorice.

"So this is our army?" Johnny said skeptically to Tag. "Nine cats and one mouse…"

"I know," replied Tag. "It wasn't easy finding anyone willing to go to Dog Castle. And for some reason, the dogs we asked seemed even more afraid than the cats…but I don't think we can waste any more time looking for more."

Johnny was a little surprised by Tag's newfound confidence. Nine cats wasn't a whole lot better than before. "Do you think we have enough?" he asked.

"No," Tag answered honestly. Then he paused and felt great grief. "But who knows what's happened to Licorice or the others already?"

Johnny shrugged in agreement. He was eager to go, however many animals they had. "We'd better leave soon," he said.

"Not tonight," Tag said. "You and Brian are already exhausted. And if we walk all night, we'll be too tired tomorrow. We'll all sleep here tonight and head out first thing in the morning."

The nine cats and one mouse went inside and ate. They knew it would be a long trip the next day and they would need all the energy they could get. After dinner, each cat used materials from around the house to assemble a holder for his or her sword, similar to the one Tag and Johnny had seen Licorice carrying. Tag also packed some food for everyone and two flashlights, and Richard took the liberty of gathering some medical supplies. The animals went to sleep early that night, trying to prepare for the task that lay ahead of them.

Back at Dog Castle, Licorice had eventually drifted into an uneasy slumber on the hard stone ground of the dungeon cell. He was awakened sometime around nightfall by the sound of the iron dungeon gate being opened and the surly voices of dogs giving orders.

Licorice regained his senses quickly, afraid that his captors were coming for him. Instead, he saw what he had been expecting earlier.

A group of eight cats was being shepherded into the dungeon area. They all had shackles on their legs, as Licorice did, and they all appeared filthy and exhausted. The scruffy-looking group of cats was marched in and locked up in the cell across from him. In a funny way, Licorice felt relieved not to be alone anymore, but he was sorry to see the cats imprisoned.

Before Licorice even thought of something to say to the other cell's occupants, a second group of cats appeared at the main dungeon gate. As that group was ushered inside, Licorice recognized one of the cats.

It was Mary! This time, Licorice's cell was opened up, and the group was shoved in with him.

"Licorice?" said Mary as she realized it was him.

Licorice was at a loss for words as they hugged each other tightly. He wished he had been able to rescue her, but for now it was enough to see that she was all right.

"Are you okay?" she asked him. She, too, had a chain connecting her hind legs.

"I'm fine," he replied. "How are you?"

"I'm okay," she answered. "But what are you doing here? Did they kidnap you, too?"

"Um, actually…I was trying to rescue you," Licorice admitted.

"You *what*?" Mary replied. Clearly, she was touched by what he had done but also mad at him for risking his life so heedlessly.

"Don't say anything," Licorice begged her, feeling embarrassed now with all the other cats listening. "I know it was a dumb idea—but I couldn't just leave you here."

Mary looked at him affectionately and sighed. "Well, at least you're all right," she said.

"Where have you been?" Licorice asked.

"Every day they take us out to look for some crystal," Mary explained. "But we haven't found it yet."

Licorice nodded affirmatively, understanding now where the cats had been all day. Mary began introducing him to the others in their cell.

While Licorice was getting acquainted with his cellmates, two more groups of prisoners returned to the dungeon, filling up the last two cells. There were approximately thirty cats in all, imprisoned in the four different cells. After all the groups had returned, the guards brought them some dinner, and the cats ate quietly.

Just as the cats were finishing their paltry meal, everyone heard a terrifying, malicious laugh from somewhere down the corridor. All of the cats looked up in fright, and even the guards in the dungeon stopped what they were doing and were silent.

General Doverman appeared first and opened up the main dungeon gate. Then a group of dogs strode in on their hind legs. There were four guards and one dog who wore a king's robe. Everyone knew it was King Wolf.

The king was a large, powerfully built, entirely white dog with fierce, unrelenting gray eyes, sharp fangs, and a sly grin. He was several years older than Licorice, very fit, and he looked as if he could defeat any of the other dogs in a swordfight. Judging by the reaction of the officers in the dungeon, it was obvious to Licorice that the other dogs either feared him, respected him, or both. It was no wonder they were afraid to betray him. Licorice watched as the guards straightened up and stood at attention in the king's presence.

The king addressed General Doverman. "Which one is he?"

"That one," the general answered, pointing to Licorice.

A sudden rush of anxiety came over Licorice as the king's heavy gaze fell upon him. The king approached the cell with a curious expression on his face.

"Well, his eyes are green," he said to the general with disappointment, "but that's about it. This scrawny cat doesn't look anything like Julius, that stubborn animal who dared to hide the

crystal from me…*Still*, only one like him would have the audacity to try to *rescue* this pathetic bunch of cats."

Suddenly, Licorice gathered up all his nerve and rage and rushed up to the bars of the cell. "Let us out of here!" he demanded.

The king was unfazed by the outburst. "Silence!" he responded sharply. "I didn't give you permission to speak."

Licorice shrank back, startled by the king's harsh tone, and the guards snickered with amusement.

Then the king's tenor changed. "Wait a minute," he began. "I know who *you* are..."

Licorice began to feel uneasy as the king's expression turned to one of recognition.

"You're one of the '*rich cats*'!"

Licorice was shocked to be identified by the king, as if the king had discovered a deep, dark secret about him. The leader of the Canine Order glared at him wickedly.

"Well, *your majesty*," the king mocked him, "if I'd have known you were coming, I wouldn't have gone to the trouble of sending my soldiers after you...I didn't think any of you cats were brave or stupid enough to try to rescue your friends—but I'm glad you did. Be ready to join the search party for the crystal at dawn!"

The other dogs growled mercilessly.

The king seemed ready to leave, but then he added one more thing. "It looks like there's more where this crazy cat came from," he announced to his followers. "I've just learned from our spies that an army of one hundred animals—led by the *other* rich cats—is on its way here."

Licorice couldn't believe his ears.

"When they arrive," the king said fiendishly, "we'll be expecting them."

The other dogs in the dungeon howled uproariously in approval and banged the butts of their spears on the ground. With a resounding chortle, the king left the dungeon, along with his guards.

Licorice looked at Mary gravely. He knew Tag and Johnny had been opposed to coming to Dog Castle, but they must have changed their minds because of him. When he had gone off by himself, his intention had been that no one else would be endangered. Now it seemed that all his friends were coming on account of him, and since King Wolf knew about it, they would certainly fall into his clutches as well. Worse still, there was nothing he could do about it.

XII
The Search Party

The next morning, the top guard roused the sleeping prisoners by raking his sword noisily across the bars of Licorice's cell.

"Wake up, you lazy cats!" he yelled. "Time for your breakfast!"

Immediately, all the cats started to crowd around the doors of their cells. The top guard unlocked Licorice's cell while a number of guards watched closely in case anyone attempted to get out. A half loaf of bread and a bowl of water were placed just inside the doorway. Then the door was shut and the guards moved on to the next cell.

The first cat to receive the bread tore off a piece and passed along the rest. Each of them was lucky to get a small serving.

Licorice sniffed at his meal suspiciously, then took a small, reluctant bite. The bread was probably stale, he determined, and it tasted even worse than it smelled. Meanwhile, the other cats, who had been held captive for a longer time, devoured their portions hungrily.

"Eat quickly!" the top guard urged them. "We leave at dawn!"

Along with several other dogs, Guarddog had just reported for duty. As a lieutenant in King Wolf's army, he was normally responsible for guarding the prisoners during the day. Today he would be joining one of the search parties.

Guarddog noticed that Licorice was not eating his bread. He discretely wandered over to his cell.

"You'd better eat that," he advised him. "You'll be gone all day, and you won't get anything else until tonight."

Since Guarddog was alone for a moment, Licorice wanted to ask him if he knew about the king's plans for the army of animals that was on its way. He stood up and gripped the bars of the cell.

"Did you hear?" he whispered. "There's an army of animals on its way here to save us."

"Yes, I know," Guarddog responded. "I—"

"Lieutenant?" Another guard was approaching to ask Guarddog a question, and the dog had to abruptly break off their conversation. He stepped away from the cell with the other dog.

Licorice understood that Guarddog could not afford to reveal his sympathy for the cats. He watched for a second with disappointment and then sat back down again. Reluctantly, he looked at his breakfast and bit into it. Eventually he finished the whole piece.

Before long, the guards returned and unlocked the cats' cells. Licorice, Mary, and the other six cats from that cell were the first to be marched out of the dungeon.

The eight cats were guided through a number of corridors and up a flight of stairs before they arrived in the entryway inside of the castle's drawbridge. Hallways to the right and left led away from this anteroom, and across from the closed, wooden drawbridge was an open courtyard. Sixteen dogs were assembled here to take out the search party. Licorice wished that Guarddog was going with them, but the dog had been assigned to a different group.

"Listen up, you cats!" called out the commanding officer in charge. "Some of you are new here, so we're going to go over the rules once again."

Licorice knew the officer was referring to him.

"You'll be taking orders from me and the other dogs here. Whatever we say, you will do. Does everyone understand?"

The rest of the cats nodded their heads to prove that they were paying attention. Licorice refused to acknowledge the commander but tried to listen closely.

The dog went on. "We'll be looking for a crystal. I don't know what it looks like, but you'll know it when you see it. If you find it, report it right away, and we'll bring it back here immediately. The king assures me that once we find it, all the cats will be freed. But if we don't find it, we'll be going out like this every day until we do. Does everyone understand?"

Once again the cats nodded. No one believed that the king would free them, even if they did find the crystal.

Licorice, meanwhile, did not hear a word the commander was saying. He had begun pondering Guarddog's words from the night they had met. What if he *was* the one the king was looking for? Certainly, neither of his parents was the one who had hidden the crystal, but what if it was some other relative of his? In any case, he silently reminded himself *not* to report anything if he found it.

"One more thing," the dog added. "If any cat disobeys or tries to escape, he or she will be executed."

The cats showed no reaction. They just looked down disconsolately and avoided eye contact with the commander.

The commander paced a few steps into the castle's courtyard and called to some officers at least a floor above them. "Lower the drawbridge!"

From somewhere overhead, the cats could hear a low rumbling accompanied by a metallic-sounding squeak. With two taut chains supporting its weight, the massive drawbridge gradually came down. It hit the ground with a low thud. Outside, the sun was just coming up.

"Move out," ordered the commander.

With soldiers marching on both sides of them, the cats headed across the drawbridge and into the forest.

The forest was foggy, and the air was fresh and cool. The cats moved among the trees and bushes, unsure of where they were headed. In fact, it did not seem that the dogs were leading them in any particular direction. Instead, the cats were left to determine the path.

Licorice noticed that the group's bearing did not seem very deliberate, but he had an idea why the cats were allowed to control the route. The king knew that one of the cats might be drawn to the crystal, so he was probably hoping that the cats would just lead the dogs to it without realizing it. Licorice stayed near the rear of the group with Mary, letting the other, more seasoned prisoners take the lead.

After the first three hours, the search party walked along at the foot of a craggy mountain. The dogs were more casual now in the way they guarded their captives. They walked further from the cats, allowing them more freedom to choose the group's course. The dogs talked amongst themselves, and the prisoner-cats had already found that they could talk to each other without any consequences.

Licorice and Mary eventually moved to the front of the group.

"Where are we going?" Licorice asked the lead cat.

"Who knows?" the cat replied with exhaustion. "Just walk as slowly as you can. The less far we go *away* from the castle, the less distance we'll have to walk *back*."

Licorice and Mary agreed and decided to let the tired cat stay in the lead.

After another two hours of walking, the sun had reached its highest point in the sky, and it had become fairly warm. At last, the dogs ordered the cats to stop and take a fifteen-minute break. The exhausted cats collapsed right where they were and rested in the grass. Meanwhile, the dogs opened up the packs they had been carrying and started to eat their lunches. The cats had nothing, but they were relieved to get a short rest.

"Now we'll start heading back," said the cat who had been leading the group.

"What do they want from us?" questioned a tired, little cat resting on a patch of weeds. The poor cat did not look like she could get up.

Licorice and the lead cat explained why King Wolf wanted the crystal and why he needed the cats to find it for him. Mary, who had not been present when Licorice first heard the story, was astonished.

Soon the break was over, and the dogs directed the cats to start walking back toward the castle. Mary and another cat went to help the little cat to her feet. The downtrodden group feebly made its way back the way it had come.

After another two hours, the group was sweaty, dirty, and much too tired to talk anymore. They trudged on speechlessly in the shadow of the mountain they had passed earlier. Luckily, the weary little cat had regained some strength and was walking on her own now.

Licorice could feel his stomach gurgling…he was starving. He began to think of eating a grand dinner back at his mansion—which made him think of Tag and Johnny, who might already be at Dog Castle trying to rescue him. If they were captured, too, he could never forgive himself.

At least, he thought, they would be back in a few hours, and no one in his group had found the crystal—King Wolf would not have the satisfaction of getting it from *this* brave group of cats. Still, he could not stop worrying about Tag and Johnny. If he could just get back to the castle in time, he imagined, maybe he could spot them and warn them somehow.

Licorice was walking quickly now, as his thoughts were running wild, but the group could not move any faster than it already was. He had just passed all the cats when suddenly the chain on his hind legs pulled tight and tripped him. He toppled awkwardly, face-first, to the ground.

Mary was quick to help him to his feet. She looked at him tenderly.

Licorice looked angrily at the chain that bound his legs, but then he noticed something. All of the links in the chain seemed very brittle, but one in particular appeared quite weak. He tried to examine it more closely before he continued walking.

"I think maybe I can break this chain," he whispered to Mary and the other cats as they moved on by him.

The others were too tired to respond, but Mary studied the chain hopefully. "Maybe if you can escape," she said, "you can go back and warn everyone that King Wolf knows they're coming."

Licorice nodded in agreement. Then, while Mary tried to keep an eye on the dogs to make sure they were not looking, he started trying to stretch the chain with every step he took. A few times, he would take two steps with his front legs and then kick his back legs up in the air, trying to split them apart. Fortunately, the dogs were not paying close attention.

Suddenly, on one kick, Licorice heard a metallic *clink* as his legs overcame the resistance of the chain. The dogs didn't seem to have noticed.

Looking back at his hind legs, Licorice could see that the chain was broken. It felt tremendous to be able to move freely once again. He looked at Mary triumphantly, but then he felt worried.

"Will you be okay?" he asked her.

"I'll be fine," she assured him. "You have to warn the others."

Licorice hated to leave Mary, but he knew what he had to do. It had been a bad idea to come to Dog Castle in the first place, and now he had to make sure things didn't get any worse. If he could just prevent the army of animals from falling into King Wolf's trap, maybe together they could find a way to rescue the rest of the cats.

"I'll see you soon," he said simply. Then he dropped to the back of the group and shrewdly observed the dogs to see if they were watching.

Just then, he decided, the time was right. He turned and sprinted in the other direction. One of the dogs spotted him and could not believe his eyes.

"Hey! Stop cat!" he alerted the others.

The commanding officer immediately dispatched four dogs to capture Licorice. They headed off into the woods after him.

As Licorice raced through the Forest, he could detect the four dogs coming up quickly behind him. Unfortunately, he had not considered how tired his legs felt after walking all day and how weak he now felt from having had so little to eat. There was no way he could outrun the guards—he would have to find someplace to hide. Hastily, he decided to head up the mountain. It seemed like there would be a lot of hiding places amongst the rocks.

Licorice turned and scrambled up a slippery slope of sand. The four pursuers reached the bottom just as he got to the top of the incline. With difficulty, he climbed over some big rocks and then went up another slope with dirt and bushes. The dogs seemed to be gaining on him.

Suddenly, Licorice urgently felt that he needed to reach the *top* of the mountain. He had more energy now, and he briefly widened his distance from the four dogs. The determined cat headed up a steep path, and the four dogs diligently stayed with him.

Licorice continued to ascend higher and higher up the mountain. He had no idea how he would elude the dogs, but if he could just reach the top, he knew everything would be okay.

Finally he came to a place where he was uncertain of the best path to take. As he paused to decide, the dogs drew dangerously close.

"Stop right there!" ordered the one in front.

Licorice turned and tried to hoist himself up a large rock, but it was too steep. He scratched desperately at the hard surface as he slid back down. The dogs grabbed him immediately.

"Let me go!" cried Licorice as he struggled madly against his captors. He had to get to the top.

"Don't make things any harder on yourself!" one of the dogs urged him.

Then, suddenly Licorice felt calm. Everything was clear now. The dogs were locking another chain around his legs, but now he was glad he had not reached the top. It was the *crystal*! The crystal was at the top of the mountain, and it had attracted him there. Just as the old cat had described, he could sense it, and it had been attracting him to it without him even realizing it. Apparently, Guarddog had been right. *He was related to the cat who had found the crystal!* How it could be possible, he had no idea, but he knew without a doubt that it was true. Somehow, just being near the crystal had made him aware of his connection to it.

Licorice was escorted back to the rest of the search party, which had stopped to wait for him and the four dogs. He could only hope that the dogs did not realize the connection between his escape attempt and the location of the crystal.

Mary's spirits sank when she saw the group approaching.

"You just made a huge mistake!" crowed the commanding officer. "Now you've made us late. I wonder what King Wolf will do..." He and the other guards chuckled callously. "Let's go," he said, "before it gets dark."

Mary looked at Licorice worriedly.

Licorice wanted to tell her what he knew, but now was not the time.

Before long, the sun began to set behind the Forest's distant mountains. After walking in the dark for about an hour, the search party saw the castle looming ahead. When the group of animals finally reached it, they found King Wolf himself on the drawbridge waiting for them, surrounded by several guards bearing torches.

"Well, commander!" the king roared. "You'd better have a good explanation for this. All the other groups returned over an hour ago."

"You, cat," the officer addressed Licorice. "Move to the front."

Licorice bravely stepped forward to face the king, and the king recognized him immediately.

"This cat tried to escape," the commander reported. "My guards had to chase him practically all the way up Mount Verity."

"This is the same cat that was captured yesterday morning—the 'rich cat'," noted the king, eyeing him closely.

"I assume he'll be executed," said the commander icily.

"That wouldn't be a good idea," the king responded surprisingly. "We might need this cat."

The commander was baffled. "Your majesty?"

The king thought some more and then questioned the commander. "How did he escape?"

"His chain broke," the commander explained nervously. "I'm sorry, I—"

"Of course…" The king began to laugh devilishly.

The commander looked confused.

Mary listened intently, not understanding what was happening.

"Don't you see?" the king said. "Amazing things have been happening to animals to bring them to that city, and this cat owns his own *mansion*. This is the only cat who came to us on his own, who we didn't capture from the town. And no ordinary cat could escape that easily. And why would he try to go *up* the mountain? It's much more difficult—and all of this happened on his *first day* in the search party."

"I don't understand," said the commander.

"You fool," said the king. "I studied the crystal for a long time, and I know how it works. Only a cat related to Julius would have all those things happen. This cat knows where the crystal is! It's near the top of Mount Verity."

Mary gasped.

Licorice's eyes opened wide, and a chill swept through his entire body. The king knew! He was about to deny it, but the commander spoke first.

"Your majesty...Are you sure?"

"Take this cat back to his cell and treat him well," ordered the king, ignoring the commander's skepticism. "Tomorrow we'll retrieve the crystal!"

The king never did ask Licorice any questions. Instead, Licorice, Mary, and the others were taken back to the dungeon. Although the king had said to treat Licorice well, he was thrown back in the cell with all the other prisoners. He received the same small amount of food as he had gotten for dinner the night before.

Licorice felt horrible. He had unwittingly led the Canine Order right to the crystal. How was he supposed to know that it was *his* family that had discovered it? If only he had listened to *someone*—Tag, Johnny, the old cat at the Cougar Club Coffee Shop, Harie, Guarddog—none of this would have happened.

Mary and the other cats were not mad at Licorice, but they were extremely concerned. By the next day, it seemed, the king would have the crystal. Then he would take over the nearby Suburb City, and who knew what else? Furthermore, once the king didn't need the prisoners to search for the crystal anymore, what would he do with them?

XIII
The Forest Dweller

In Suburb City that same day, the army of animals woke up early and had breakfast. When everyone was finished and ready to leave, they all gathered outside on the mansion's porch with their swords and supplies. Since Tag had done most of the recruiting, the other animals looked to him for direction.

Tag hesitated at first. When he had assembled the army, he hadn't entirely considered that he would also be *leading* it. The one thing he knew was that these were his truest friends here. Even though they needed every animal they could get, he should give each of them a final chance to change their mind.

"First of all," he began, "Johnny and I want to thank everyone for helping us on this journey. None of us knows what's going to happen, but once we get started…there's no turning back. If anyone wants to change their mind, now is your last chance."

The others all looked around at each other, wondering if anyone would take the opportunity, but no one seemed to be moving or saying anything. If anything, they seemed to appreciate the thoughtfulness of Tag's offer.

Tag realized that no one was backing out. "Okay," he said resolutely. "Let's go."

Off the cats went, heading for the Animals' Forest and Dog Castle.

The army of animals reached the Forest in the late morning, and as soon as they entered, they experienced the same effects that Licorice had felt. Their swords seemed lighter to them, and they, too, could walk easily on their hind legs. The place seemed familiar to them, like something from a dream or a forgotten memory, but it was the first time there for each of them.

Unfortunately, the benefits of being in the Forest did not help the cats feel any less nervous. Except for Tag and Johnny, none of them had ever faced the sort of danger they were expecting, and several had expressed concern about how they would perform when the time came.

After walking for a while, the cats decided to split up into two groups to search for a trail. They would meet back at a particularly tall tree that would be easy to see from anywhere. Tag led one group, which included Softy, Mandy, Richard, and Whitey; Johnny led the other group, which included April, Brian, Ben, and Blackey.

Tag's group had not gone far before it came to a sparsely vegetated area with rows of shedding, autumn trees on both sides. The ground was covered with red, brown, orange, and yellow leaves.

"Maybe *this* is a trail," suggested Whitey.

Tag agreed and replied, "Let's check it out."

With Softy leading the way a few feet ahead of them, the four cats followed the leafy path. The soil was still damp from previous rain showers, but the freshly fallen leaves were dry, breaking apart crisply as the cats treaded upon them. Because the tree branches protruded over them and partially blocked the sun, the area was quite shady. Aside from the cats' paws crunching on the dry leaves, the forest seemed very quiet and still.

Suddenly, without any warning, the cats felt the ground give way underneath them. Before they knew it, they were falling! All four cats hit ground at the bottom of a deep pit.

Only Softy remained safely above ground. He turned back and peered over the edge of what had been a camouflaged trap. Apparently, he had not been heavy enough to trigger the trap.

"Tag! Mandy!" he called out. "Whitey? Richard?"

All four cats appeared unconscious.

Then Softy heard a loud grunt emanating from somewhere in the forest. He could detect movement amongst the trees, and it was getting closer. He heard another loud grunt, which seemed much closer now.

Before Softy could do anything, a giant shadow was looming over him. It was an enormous caveman! Softy was paralyzed with fear.

The caveman was not concerned with a tiny mouse. With astonishing speed, the oversized human approached the pit and climbed down inside it. A moment later, with equal adeptness, he hoisted himself back up to the surface. With all four cats and their belongings tucked securely under one of his mighty arms, the caveman headed off into the forest. Softy could only follow.

Before long, the caveman reached an opening in the side of a rocky hill and headed inside. Softy followed him down a dark corridor. Soon it became lighter, but the source of the light was not sunshine; it was fire from a torch wedged between some rocks at the entryway to a large chamber.

Softy peered into what was evidently the caveman's living space. Scattered about the shadowy den was a peculiar collection of primitive tools, along with some more modern objects. There were rocks in the shape of spearheads, wooden sticks of varying lengths, and various bones and fur from animals. There were also some metallic utensils, pots, and pans that Softy assumed must have come from the city. A total of four torches were propped up in rock piles around the edges of the chamber, keeping it aglow. The cats' swords and packs had been dropped in a pile not far from the entrance. Leaning against the wall was a giant club.

In the torch-lit chamber, Softy noticed that the caveman had extremely long black hair, including his beard and mustache. He wore the skin of an animal as clothing.

In the center of the area was a giant cauldron filled with water. The caveman used one of the torches to ignite a fire underneath it and held the helpless cats above it by their tails.

It was then that Richard began to wake up. He was still feeling quite groggy, but his eyes opened wide as he focused on the water underneath him. He quickly discovered that he was hanging upside down.

As soon as Richard realized what was happening, he began shaking the others, trying to awaken them. One by one they regained consciousness, and they all looked at the caveman in fright. They tried to scratch at him with their claws, but he was holding them too far out of reach. The caveman was using his free hand to sprinkle some herbs and spices into the water.

"What's he doing?" asked Mandy, who wasn't sure she wanted an answer.

"I think he's making his lunch!" replied Richard in terror.

The caveman dropped the four cats into the water, and immediately they started splashing with their paws, trying to keep themselves afloat. The water was still cool, but they knew it would get hotter.

Softy, who had remained unnoticed by the caveman, shrieked. He turned and ran for help.

"Heeelp!" Whitey cried at the top of his lungs. Desperately he clawed at the side of the giant pot, trying to pull himself up, but the surface was too smooth and the lip of the pot too far out of reach. His paws slid limply back down into the water.

The helpless cats screamed and yelped as the water began to heat up.

Softy raced through the dense woods in search of Johnny's group when suddenly he heard the distinct hoot of a hungry owl. The frightened mouse scooted over to some nearby bushes just as the large bird dove down at him. The owl landed on top of the bushes and started prodding at them with his bill. Then Softy made a break for it. The owl was slow to see him, but continued the chase, gaining on Softy every minute.

Meanwhile, Johnny's group had found a trail and had returned to the designated tree. Some of them wandered nearby, exploring the area, while they waited for Tag's group.

Just then, Softy skidded into the cats' view. He was puffing and panting as the owl swooped down. Brian picked up Softy just in time, and the owl landed on a limb of the big tree. Brian handed Softy to Johnny, and the owl promptly became discouraged and left.

Standing up in Johnny's two paws, Softy imparted his news. "Tag, Mandy, Whitey, and Richard are in a cave. A caveman's got them!"

The others gathered around.

"A what?" said Johnny. Then he remembered—Tag and Licorice had told him that there were supposed to be primitive humans in the Animals' Forest.

"A caveman!" Softy repeated urgently.

April and Blackey looked at each other with concern, realizing that their friends were already in danger, and they hadn't even reached Dog Castle yet.

"Okay, lead us there," said Johnny. He put Softy down.

"Follow me!" said Softy. He hurried through the Animals' Forest, followed closely by the cats.

Back at the old cave, the caveman was adding more wood to the fire. The four cats were almost drowning in the cauldron, and the water was getting uncomfortably warm.

Just then, the four cats heard what sounded like voices. They looked at each other hopefully and tried to be quiet so they could hear. They had to keep paddling, though, to keep their heads up.

The voices seemed to be getting closer, but then they stopped. The cats heard the sound of rapidly scuttling feet on the dank cave floor.

The wily caveman heard the sounds, too. He took hold of his club and hid behind a rock formation near the chamber's entrance.

Johnny's group came rushing in. Immediately they saw the large cauldron and the fire underneath it.

"Whitey!" exclaimed Blackey.

Hearing Blackey's voice, the cats in the pot cried out. The hulking caveman rose up from behind the rock.

The five cats looked up in fright as the caveman swung his heavy club. Ben pulled Blackey out of the way and April shoved Johnny clear as they all dove in different directions. The club smashed into the ground with a loud whack.

The caveman chased after one cat, then another. Unseen by the caveman, Softy scurried over to a bowl carved out of stone that was filled with water. With a great effort, he pushed the bowl closer to the fire. Then he tipped it over. The water put out part of the fire, but not all of it.

Meanwhile, the caveman approached Brian and Blackey. The two cats readied their swords, but the caveman, with a single swing of his club, knocked the swords away from both of them. Then Ben, without really thinking about the consequences, used his sword and poked the caveman in the rump. The caveman howled with pain and went after him.

"Help the others while I distract him!" yelled Ben.

"We can stand on each other's backs," April told the other three cats.

The four of them gathered near the cauldron. Johnny carefully stood on Blackey's back, and Brian immediately stepped up above him. Then April carefully climbed to the top of the stack, enabling her to reach their comrades in the deep pot.

"Hurry up," said Blackey uncomfortably, from the bottom of the pile.

One by one, April helped the sopping wet cats out of the pot, and each of them leaped to the ground with relief. They all rushed for the exit and retrieved their swords from the pile there.

"Come on, Ben!" Johnny urged his friend. The cats and Softy all called for Ben to come, but the caveman had him cornered. He raked the sword from Ben's paw.

Tag was welling with resentment toward the caveman for capturing him and his friends. Once he had a hold of his sword, he let out a holler and charged bitterly at his former captor. Unfortunately, the caveman was alerted by the cry—with a contemptuous grunt and a backhanded swing of his arm, he swatted Tag like a pesky insect, knocking him squarely into the wall. Tag was dazed, but before he knew it, Mandy and April were there, helping him to his feet and guiding him back toward the chamber's entrance.

Then Brian had an idea. "The torches!" he shouted. The nearest one was too high to reach with his paw, so he quickly swung his sword at it, knocking it to the ground. He then scooped it up and tossed it into the pot of water, extinguishing the flame.

Immediately the chamber was darker, but there were still three more torches. The caveman swung at Ben with his arm, but Ben leaped out of the way.

Johnny, Richard, and Whitey followed Brian's example and went for the remaining torches. The three cats used their swords to dislodge them and, one by one, picked them up and threw them into the water. The chamber became almost pitch dark, except for the small flame flickering underneath the cauldron. The three cats felt their way back toward the others, tripping over the caveman's things—and each other—in the dark.

Barely able to see Ben anymore, the caveman swung his club wildly but missed. Ben ran forward, only to bump into the caveman's leg. Knowing where Ben was now, the caveman tried to grab him, but Ben was too quick. He darted between the caveman's legs and felt his hind leg kick painfully into something metallic. Wincing, he grasped his sword from the ground and sprinted toward his waiting friends.

The caveman, who was quite incensed, went after all of them. The cats grabbed the rest of their things and hurried back up the cave's entryway. The first few seconds seemed like an eternity, but finally they saw the bright mouth of the cave up ahead. The cats emerged from the caveman's lair and headed out into the open forest. At the cave entrance, the caveman hollered, jumped up and down, and stomped the ground with fury.

Once they reached the trail Johnny's group had found, the cats rested and drank from a nearby stream. Ben washed a mild cut on his leg, which he had received when he had bumped into his sword. Then Richard helped him wrap it with some of the bandages he had brought. Tag, Mandy, Richard, and Whitey were still a bit soaked, but they were grateful to have remained uncooked. They were sure to thank their friends for saving them.

The stories about the Animals' Forest were quite accurate, concluded Tag and Johnny—even, as Ralph and Daisy had mentioned, the part about primitive humans. At least they'd had their first taste of action, Mandy pointed out. It was hard to say how much the magic of the Animals' Forest had helped them, but whatever the reason, the cats felt more confident now. They had proven that they could act bravely in a perilous situation. Luckily, they hadn't lost anyone in the process.

Of all the cats, though, Tag was the only one who felt less confident. Some leader he was, he thought to himself. They had only been in the Forest for a few hours, and already he had almost gotten half the group eaten by a caveman.

Unfortunately, the cats' encounter with the caveman, including their recuperation by the stream, had cost them several hours. It was already mid afternoon by the time they were under way again. The sun was getting low in the sky and the air was beginning to feel cool, but the cats took solace knowing that they were all together and on the trail. They were not sure which direction to *follow* the trail, so they had taken their best guess.

After about an hour, the cats encountered one of the Forest's signs pointing to Dog Castle. It turned out they had been traveling in the wrong direction; they would have to turn around and go back the way they had come.

Although no one could have known which way to go, Tag felt more disheartened now as the leader of the group. It had already cost them an hour going the wrong way, and it would take them another hour to re-cover their tracks. He couldn't help feeling responsible.

The group followed the trail as twilight and darkness fell upon the Forest. The cats were tired, but they continued onward for several more hours. Eventually the clouds rolled in and it started to sprinkle lightly, making all the cats cold and uncomfortable.

"We'll never get there at this rate," said Richard, but as April glanced ahead, she knew he was wrong.

"Look!" she exclaimed.

In the distance, enshrouded in a cloak of ghostly fog, was Dog Castle. The whole group was silent for a moment, transfixed by the terrifying structure.

Tag could see that the group was tired and also a bit demoralized. "It's getting late," he stated. "I think we should get some rest. Let's set up camp."

The group found a secluded area away from the trail where it could remain hidden until morning. After eating a quick, soggy dinner, the animals lay down to go to sleep, except for Ben and Blackey, who had volunteered for the first guard shift.

Everyone in the group was a bit edgy, but they eventually fell into a light sleep. The next day, they all knew, would be the challenge of their lives.

Inside the castle, Guarddog had been thinking all day about the army of animals and the king's plans for them. Finally, he decided that he really needed to see his friend, Harie. He had visited Harie before, but never by going out the window and climbing down the tree—for two reasons. First, if the other dogs discovered that he was sneaking out, he would be in big trouble; and second, he was dreadfully afraid of heights. That night, though, he bravely looked down into the moat below and hopped out to the tree branch. Clinging tightly to the branches for dear life, he secretly climbed down the tree and ventured out into the forest to seek out his friend.

XIV

The Passageway

The next morning, as the now cloudless sky shone black with just a trace of indigo, the army of animals was on its way again. The nine cats and one mouse marched toward the menacing Dog Castle, not quite sure how they would accomplish their objective but determined to try. Unknown to them, someone was following them and watching them from amongst the trees.

As the animals neared their target, they tried to remain concealed amongst the Forest's vegetation. Hiding behind a thicket of bushes, they examined the fortress's exterior. There were no dogs on patrol outside the castle and no lookouts visible anywhere. The drawbridge was wide open.

"There's no one watching," observed Mandy.

"Yeah," whispered Ben, "let's go in now while we have the chance." They both looked toward Tag to see what he thought.

Tag hesitated—he hadn't expected to just walk right in. He could see that all the cats were ready and waiting for him to give the word, but something felt funny to him about the situation…Maybe he had just lost his nerve…

Tag was about to respond when they all heard a rustling sound. Suddenly, a large rabbit with floppy ears bounded in from the underbrush.

"Wait!" whispered the rabbit. "You can't go in there!"

The cats were startled at first, especially seeing that he had a sword, but they quickly realized that he was alone.

"Who are you?" questioned Johnny, lowering his blade.

"My name's Harie," the rabbit answered, "and I'm here to help you—where's the rest of your army?"

Tag and Johnny looked at each other, puzzled. How could the rabbit have known they were coming?

The rabbit seemed quite confused that there were no other animals with them, but he went on. "King Wolf knows you're coming. He *wants* you to try to get in."

"Why do you say that?" asked Tag.

"The drawbridge was left open on purpose. All the soldiers are waiting inside the castle. Their plan is to let you come in and then close it behind you and trap you. My friend, Guarddog, lives in the castle, and he told me that some spies found out. He said there was an army of over one hundred animals on its way and asked me to help you get into the castle."

"Those two dogs in the alley…," Ben said to Tag, realizing where the Canine Order had gotten its information—which was not completely correct.

"If your friend lives in Dog Castle, why would he want to help *us*?" questioned Mandy.

"Well, he doesn't really support King Wolf," Harie explained. "Plus, I think he and I met one of your friends."

"You met Licorice?" Johnny said.

"A black cat, with a speck of white on his chest?"

"That's him!" squeaked Softy.

"Well, he was captured," said Harie, confirming the cats' worries, "but not until after he met my friend, Guarddog. For some reason, Guarddog really wants to help your friend—and all the other cats."

"Well, this is our whole army," Tag informed the rabbit.

Harie paused for a minute and then sighed. "It'll have to do... There's another way we can get in," he explained, "a back door."

"There's a *back* door?" questioned Johnny.

"The king held me prisoner for a while, but my friend Guarddog secretly helped me escape through it. A passageway leads to it underneath the moat, and it's locked from the inside. Guarddog told me he would have it unlocked by this morning. It'll get us pretty close to the dungeon, but the problem will be getting back out."

Tag felt reassured. His instincts had been right not to charge across the open drawbridge, and assuming they could trust the rabbit, sneaking in through a secret entrance not far from the dungeon was a much better plan.

"Let's go," he said confidently.

As the sky grew lighter, Harie led the group back out into the woods. They took a winding route away from the castle and eventually approached it from the rear.

The rabbit slowed down and scrutinized the area closely. He spotted a group of shrubs and moved towards it. Hastily he removed a number of branches and leaves, which had actually been covering up a pair of wooden doors set almost horizontally with the ground.

Not knowing what to expect, the cats readied their swords, and Harie and Ben swung back the pair of doors. Peering inside, the group could see a dark, sloping path. The sides were mostly wood, and the ground was a combination of dirt and stone.

"It's awfully dark in there," Richard murmured nervously.

"Stay behind me," Blackey told his brother, Whitey.

Tag retrieved the two flashlights from his pack and handed one to Johnny. The two cats turned the flashlights on and aimed them down into the passage. Carefully, Harie pressed his paws against the sides for support and ventured down inside. One at a time, the cats followed.

Brian was the last one. Thoughtfully he took the time to close each of the doors behind them in order to better conceal their presence. As soon as the doors were closed, the passage became nearly pitch dark.

The corridor was fairly narrow, only wide enough for two animals to walk side by side. Tag and Johnny aimed the flashlights ahead and led the way.

The gloomy tunnel continued downward for several yards before leveling out. Cobwebs and roots from bushes protruded into the passageway. It was impossible to see anything except for where Tag and Johnny aimed the lights.

Soon the ground they encountered was moist, and the walls and ceiling of the passage appeared to be damp. Drips of water plopped into murky puddles on the earthen floor. The cats guessed that they must be passing underneath the moat. Eventually the ground became dry again.

Soon after that, the flashlight beams revealed the end of the tunnel. Tag, Johnny, and Harie pressed their paws against a brick wall.

"Here we are," said Harie. "There's a secret door here. Hopefully Guarddog had a chance to unlock it like he planned."

"How do we know there isn't anyone on the other side?" questioned Mandy from behind them.

No one answered until at last Johnny spoke up.

"We don't."

Tag, Johnny, and Harie looked at each other with unspoken consensus. Together, they leaned into the wall and tried to push on it...but nothing happened. The three of them paused for a second and then tried again with more effort.

This time the wall gave way a bit. A pair of cracks was revealed, with the wall slightly indented on the right side and slightly protruding on the left. The three animals pushed again on the right side. This time, the wall rotated sharply about a center point, moving away from them on the right and towards them on the left. Johnny had to step back to make room for the wall turning towards him, and now the rotating panel of bricks was aligned with the passageway, allowing entry on either side of it into a candle-lit corridor.

Poking their heads through on the right and left, Tag and Johnny surveyed the corridor and found that it was clear. The group quickly started to pass through on both sides of the turned bricks. Tag received the other flashlight from Johnny and placed them both back in his pack. He noted the various barrels and crates against the walls of the corridor. They seemed to be in a storage area.

As soon as the last of them was inside, the cats pushed again and sealed up the panel like it had been before. The bricks

blended in perfectly with the surrounding part of the wall, with only a tiny keyhole to indicate that there might be something there.

"This way," Harie urged the cats, already proceeding ahead warily.

The group quickly crept down the corridor. They knew there was no place to hide should a dog happen to come around the corner. Once any dog discovered them, their task would become much more difficult.

Tag and Harie were the first to reach the intersection with the next corridor. Together, they took a careful peek. There was no one there. Tag motioned for everyone to follow, and the intrepid group moved ahead.

Suddenly, from another corridor, a group of six dogs strolled around the corner. They were more surprised than the cats.

"Intruders!" exclaimed one of them.

Ben cried out and was the first to charge toward the unsuspecting group of dogs. He immediately began sword fighting with the first one he reached. The rest of the group was not far behind, and Tag, Johnny, Mandy, Harie, and Whitey were the first ones to engage the other five dogs.

Swords clashed as the cats tried to overpower the soldiers before any others showed up. As the other members of their group came up to help, the cats were able to force back the smaller group of dogs. Soon the outnumbered dogs took off running down the corridor. Ben was close at their heels, swatting madly at them with his sword.

"Cats in the base! Cats in the base!" hollered one of the fleeing dogs.

The cats followed the dogs to the next intersection. The dogs turned right and Ben stayed right behind them. Harie, however, paused in the middle of the intersection, recollected for half a second, and then headed left.

"Ben!" yelled Tag, to stop his friend from continuing on. Ben skidded to a stop, looked back, and saw all his friends going the other way.

The cats took the path to the left, which led them along a wide, curving corridor. Now Ben was behind all of them, but he caught up quickly.

Finally, the cats could see up ahead a large wall of iron bars, and they knew they had reached the dungeon. Unfortunately, there were sixteen dogs barring the way. Next to the gate, there was a set of keys hanging from a hook.

The officer in charge was Guarddog. As soon as he saw Harie and the cats, he gave a command. "All soldiers…lower your weapons and leave the area immediately!"

The band of cats paused briefly to see what would happen. Four of the guards obeyed Guarddog's order without question and trotted past the cats without attacking them.

"What?!" replied the second-in-command as he saw them go. "What are you talking about?"

The remaining dungeon guards looked at each other with confusion, unsure of what to do.

"He's a traitor!" realized the second-in-command. "Prepare for battle!"

The remaining guards lined up quickly and prepared to take on the invading cats. The second-in-command swung his sword at Guarddog, who was ready for him and blocked the attack with ease.

The cats rushed forward to challenge the befuddled guards. Ben and Whitey, charging forward recklessly, were the first to reach them. Johnny, dashing forward confidently, was right behind them.

"Whitey! Be careful!" called Blackey, as he and the rest of the cats met their opponents. The dogs' and cats' swords clanged against each other as each cat challenged one dog. Quickly the melee spread from wall to wall in the confined space.

Inside the dungeon, the cats could hear and partially see through the gate the commotion outside. Licorice knew it was Tag and Johnny.

"Tag! Johnny! We're here!" he called out. The other prisoners chimed in also, standing up against the bars of their cells and screaming for the others to come save them.

Tag and Mandy were at one end of the dungeon gate, facing a pair of fierce dogs. Suddenly, one of the dogs knocked Mandy's sword away from her. She stumbled to her side as the dog prepared to stab her. Then Softy was there, grabbing onto the dog's leg. At first the dog did not realize what was happening, but before he knew it, he was hopping up and down and falling over.

Seeing that Mandy was temporarily free, Tag called to her. "Try to get the keys!"

Mandy nodded in acknowledgement and ran past several distracted animals to the other end of the gate.

Meanwhile, Tag's opponent swung for his neck. At the same time, Tag ducked down, avoiding the attack and also picking up the sword that Mandy had dropped. Just as Mandy's opponent was getting to his feet, Tag threw the sword to her. She caught the sword and swiftly blocked another attack by that dog.

As the rest of the cats continued to battle the guards, Tag drove back the dog he was facing. Finally, that dog bumped into the dog facing Mandy, and they both fell over. Now Mandy had a chance to grab the keys. As the two dogs got up, Tag took a position between them and Mandy. He held off both dogs while Mandy tried the different keys in the lock.

"Hurry!" Tag urged Mandy as he struggled against both opponents.

"I'm trying...," Mandy replied with frustration.

Finally she was able to swing open the large door of iron bars. She hurried inside the dungeon and saw all of the imprisoned cats. She approached the first cell and opened it. By now, Tag had been forced back into the dungeon with her.

Even though the freed cats still had chains on their hind legs, they made their best speed toward the dogs fighting Tag. Before those two dogs knew it, each of them was knocked over by two or three of the frenzied felines and had his sword taken away. Once they had been disarmed, Tag pointed his sword at them and held them at bay.

As soon as the first group of prisoners had finished with those two dogs, they rushed toward the soldiers outside the dungeon. They jumped on the dogs' backs, covered their eyes, and helped the other cats seize their swords. Before long, all the guards were disarmed and under the cats' control.

Meanwhile, Mandy had been busy opening up the other cells. The last cell she opened was the one holding Licorice and Mary.

Mary was the first one out. She hugged her friend and thanked her as well. Licorice then emerged from the cell and did the same thing. They both saw the rest of their friends directing the now weaponless guards into the gated area. Licorice was eager to tell Tag what he knew about the crystal.

There were four more keys at the end of the dungeon. A few cats quickly got them and started unlocking the chains on everyone's legs. Guarddog ordered the captured dogs into one of the cells that had been occupied by the cats.

"You'll never get away with this," snarled the second-in-command, but Guarddog ignored him. He summoned Mandy to come over and lock the cell.

Amongst all the newly freed cats, Licorice made his way toward his brother. There was no time for pleasantries—as soon as they made eye contact, he just started talking. "*We're* the cats," he announced bluntly, "—the cats who are related to the cat who hid the crystal."

"*What?*" Tag responded as they stood face to face.

The others around them were just as astounded. Guarddog glanced at Licorice with alarm.

"*We're the cats*," Licorice repeated. "It's all the way up the mountain, and I just wanted to get up there so badly, and…my chain broke, and I tried to run up there and…King Wolf…he knows!"

Tag didn't know what to make of his brother's claim—the information was overwhelming. All he knew was that there was no time to deal with it now.

Standing right next to them, Harie spoke to Guarddog with urgency. "We'd better be fast—some guards battled us on the way in here."

"He's right," Guarddog alerted all the cats. "It won't take long for reinforcements to get here."

"We'll discuss this later," Tag told his brother, and Licorice nodded in agreement.

As the cats distributed the swords taken from the guards, Licorice turned his attention to Guarddog, realizing the difficult choice he had made.

"Thanks for helping us," he told the dog and his friend the rabbit, "but I'm sure you won't be able to live here anymore."

"I would rather die than stay in this place," said Guarddog stoutly. "But don't thank us yet—first we've got to get out of here."

XV
The Drawbridge

66 This way!" Tag urged the group of over forty animals as he led them up the curving hall away from the dungeon. So far, at least, there were no opposing troops in sight. The cats without swords stayed close to those with swords.

"Is this your whole army?" Guarddog asked Tag, recognizing him as the leader of the cats' group.

"This is it," Tag responded.

Guarddog nodded his head back and forth. "You're just as crazy as Licorice."

"He's my brother," Tag said simply.

Guarddog glanced at Licorice, who nodded his head to agree that it was true.

"No wonder," Guarddog replied.

The animals turned right at the first intersection, and before long, they had arrived at the corridor with the secret exit. It almost looked like they would make it, but at the end of the corridor, a contingent of troops was approaching fast.

"Stop them!" ordered the commander as soon as he saw the group. The soldiers charged forwards.

"Get the door open," Guarddog told Tag, "—and get as many cats out as you can." He rushed forward bravely, grabbing the nearby supply crates and shoving them into the dogs' path. Several of the cats followed his example, helping to position the crates and also turning barrels on their sides and rolling them towards the dogs. Johnny, Harie, Ben, and several members of the rescue party helped Guarddog battle with the soldiers as they came around and over the obstacles, but the larger group of dogs was forcing them back quickly.

Tag, Brian, and Richard pushed on the wall and opened the passage. Since the tunnel was very narrow, only two cats at a time would be able to enter.

The cats without swords were the first ones. Two by two they entered the passage and disappeared out of sight.

"Run as fast as you can," Tag instructed them all. "Don't stop until you get back to the city."

By the time all the unarmed cats had entered the passageway, Guarddog and the others had been forced back to where the door was.

"We can't all get out this way," Harie declared. "We'll have to find another way."

The rest of the group continued fighting, trying to give the escaping cats time to flee. Guarddog looked at Richard, who was now the closest to the door.

"Get in there," he told him.

Richard took notice of which cats were still left inside the castle. There were only a few of the former prisoners, including Licorice and Mary, and the members of the rescue party. "We all came in together, we'll all leave together," he said bravely.

"Too late now...," muttered Guarddog as the soldiers pushed them all back past the secret door. A few of the dogs entered the passageway to pursue the escaping prisoners, but the fleeing cats had a good head start over them.

Tag realized there was nothing more they could do here. "Retreat!" he directed everyone, looking the other way.

The cats turned and ran, and the dogs gave chase. As the cats fled from the hostile soldiers behind them, suddenly another unit of dogs was in view straight ahead.

"This way!" determined Johnny, heading toward an empty corridor to their right. The cats hurried along the corridor, led by Johnny, Blackey, and Whitey. Tag, Harie, Guarddog, and Ben trailed a bit behind. The two groups of dogs joined together to form a group of over forty chasing them.

"How are we going to get out of here?" questioned April.

"The only other way out is through the front!" called Guarddog, "—across the drawbridge!"

"Which way is that?" Johnny shouted back.

"Not this way!" replied Guarddog.

"Which way?" questioned Johnny, as they approached the next intersection.

"Go left!" Guarddog called, trying to look ahead.

"Okay…," Johnny replied uncertainly, turning left and heading up an especially narrow corridor.

It was impossible to see where the dimly lit corridor led. For a moment it looked as though it might be empty, but suddenly five dogs were there ahead of them, ready and waiting.

The five dogs held their ground in the narrow corridor. Johnny fearlessly took on the first one, who parried his first blow. He then blocked the dog's strike and counterattacked with a thrust. The dog avoided that and tried to swat his hind legs. Johnny leaped into the air and came down with an attack to the dog's shoulder. The dog blocked it solidly.

At the same time, the dogs behind the group had caught up. Tag, Harie, and Guarddog did their best to hold off the lead dogs. Fortunately, the corridor was too narrow for the rest to join in the combat.

In front, Johnny, Blackey, and Whitey battled the dogs with extraordinary moves, but it was obvious that the cats were going nowhere. Although there were only five dogs blocking the way, that was more than enough in the tight passage.

Guarddog tried to look over his shoulder. "There should be a stairway!" he called to Johnny, "—somewhere to your right!"

Johnny looked past the attacking dogs as well as he could, but there was no stairway in sight. "I don't see anything!" he informed the dog.

"There's a secret door," called Guarddog. "Look for a stone at the base of the wall, and step on it."

Then April, who was behind Johnny, realized that the stone was right next to her. "There it is!" she exclaimed.

While Johnny, Blackey, and Whitey fought with determination to hold their position, April pressed her paw on the stone. Instantly part of the wall receded and then slid sideways, revealing a steep stairway. April headed up the steps, followed by the others.

Softy waited at the base of the stairs for Tag or Licorice to pick him up, but he could see that Johnny, Blackey, and Whitey would have a difficult time getting free to go up the stairs themselves. Just as he had expected, Licorice came along and scooped him up, but then Softy knew what he needed to do. He leaped off Licorice's forearm and headed back down the stairs.

"Softy, wait!" Licorice yelled.

It was too late. Softy raced toward the menacing dogs and started tripping them. Licorice, who was stuck on the stairs as all the cats came up towards him, watched in admiration.

First the dog facing Johnny fell, and then the one facing Blackey. Both times Softy was nearly landed upon, but with those two dogs on the floor, the rest were blocked from attacking anyone. The dog in front tried to get up, but Johnny pushed him, knocking him over again along with a third dog.

Softy could no longer be seen amongst the fallen dogs and their swords. As the rest of the group passed behind him, Johnny looked desperately to find his friend. Then he could see that one of the dogs had him by the tail! Johnny swung his sword at the dog, forcing him to block. As the dog defended himself, he released Softy. Just as Tag, Harie, and Guarddog finally caught up, Johnny was able to pick up Softy and head up the stairs along with them. Licorice was relieved as soon as he saw Softy with Johnny.

The group emerged from the stairway into the open courtyard in the center of the castle. There were many obstacles here for combat training, such as wooden beams to balance on, walls to climb over, and trenches to jump across. There were also several targets against the wall for spear-throwing practice and an open area for military exercises.

Guarddog was the last to reach the top of the stairs, and immediately he hit another stone next to the wall with his paw. Another door slid from the side, blocking the pursuing dogs. Guarddog then wedged his sword in between the stone and the wall, which jammed the door shut. Unfortunately, now he did not have a sword.

Across the courtyard, a whole squadron of dogs was assembled in front of the castle's antechamber, and in command of the squadron was General Doverman. The general had not expected the escaped prisoners to be coming up out of the stairwell in the courtyard, but once he caught sight of them, he alerted his troops. "There they are!"

The soldiers, who were eager for action, drew their swords and rushed toward the cats.

Peering past the advancing soldiers, everyone could see that the drawbridge was *up* now. Guarddog exchanged glances with Harie, then spoke to Tag.

"If you can get to the drawbridge, we'll get it open."

"Okay," Tag replied firmly.

"But we'll need two cats to help us," Guarddog added, starting toward a curving staircase in the nearest corner of the courtyard.

Licorice overheard them and knew what he had to do. "I'll go!" he declared.

"Me, too!" announced Mary from several yards away.

"Come on!" Harie urged both of them.

The two cats followed Harie and Guarddog toward the stairs. At the same time, the rest of the group was caught up in battle with the soldiers from the courtyard.

Tag knew he couldn't stop Licorice and Mary; *someone* had to go with the dog and the rabbit. Instead, he pushed away a fierce dog and tried to head toward the entry chamber.

"Try to keep moving!" he urged the others. "It's our only chance!"

The group of cats fought bravely, fending off numerous attacks. Gradually they were able to move ahead, each of them taking a different winding route through the dogs' training area. Although the dogs tended to be stronger, the cats were quicker and more agile. They smartly kept running, ducking, and changing direction, using the various barriers as protection and sword fighting only when necessary.

As he made his way through the chaotic courtyard, Tag could not help but wonder if he would ever have another chance to talk to Licorice about the crystal.

Licorice, Mary, Harie, and Guarddog hurried up the stairs, but there was one dog rushing just as quickly downwards. As soon as he saw Licorice he prepared to swing his sword at him, but Guarddog was able to grab his paws first. As they wrestled for the weapon, Guarddog realized that this was one of his trusted friends. He knew for a fact that this dog did not support King Wolf either.

"Clarence! My friend!" said Guarddog as they stared each other in the face. "Help us escape!" Licorice, Mary, and Harie had stopped and were waiting for him several stairs above.

Clarence was a plain, white dog with brown eyes. He was neither as big nor as skillful as Guarddog.

"Sorry, Guarddog," the dog replied. "The king…"

"You don't want to be here," Guarddog tried to convince him. "Now is the time! You can escape with us!"

"You'll never make it. And if the king finds out…"

Guarddog knew there wasn't time for a discussion. These dogs had been serving King Wolf for so long that they could barely imagine living any other way. Knowing he was stronger than his friend, Guarddog yanked the sword away from him. He pushed the other dog away and moved on.

Meanwhile, General Doverman saw the animals on the stairs and ordered four nearby soldiers to go after them.

As the cats below hurried toward the entry chamber, they could see the imposing drawbridge in front of them. There were no soldiers in the way—just the large, wooden barrier preventing their escape.

The cats had no choice but to run up into the entryway, where they would have to hold their ground until their friends could lower the drawbridge. Instead of continuing to attack them, though, the dogs from the courtyard gathered a few yards back and waited. The cats were surprised by this tactic at first—until they glanced to their right and left. The corridors to both sides were also filled with dogs. The group was surrounded.

As they climbed the stairs, passing the second level of the huge fortress, Guarddog realized that Licorice was one of the two cats who had volunteered to go with him. "You shouldn't be coming with us," Guarddog said to him with alarm.

"Why not?" questioned Licorice, not understanding.

"You know where the crystal is—and so does King Wolf. You're the only one who can find it before he does—and we may not make it out of here."

Licorice had not thought of that. Only a little while ago, he had been locked up in a prison cell without much hope of ever getting out. The dog might be right, he thought, but it was too late to turn back now.

"Then we'll just have to make sure we *do* get out of here," he replied, with a tone of confidence that surprised even him.

As soon as Licorice, Mary, Harie, and Guarddog reached the top of the stairs, they dashed across the upper level toward an area directly above the entry chamber, where their friends below were surrounded. There they saw a window with a view of the outside forest. There were two large wheels here, each with a chain wound around it, and a long wooden lever sticking up from a notch in the floor. Each of the chains extended through a two-foot-wide opening in the wall. There were also two dogs, who drew their swords.

Harie and Guarddog raced decisively towards them, knowing they had to work quickly. At the same time, Licorice and Mary saw the four dogs who had come up the steps after them.

"Hurry," Mary urged the dog and the rabbit.

With three elegant moves, Guarddog had removed one of their opponents' swords. He picked it up and flung it over the ledge into the courtyard. As Harie contended with the other dog, Guarddog was able to rush up and grab that one's sword. He sent it hurling into the courtyard as well.

"Get out of here!" Guarddog fiercely threatened the two unarmed dogs. The two of them looked at each other, apparently surprised to see that Guarddog was against them, and then turned and ran.

The dog and the rabbit went to the wheels. Simultaneously they began turning them, and the heavy chains began to move. At the same time, Licorice and Mary had engaged all four approaching dogs but were being forced back quickly.

Two stories below, General Doverman had just stepped to the front of the group of dogs in the courtyard.

"Drop your weapons, cats!" he ordered.

Then they all heard a sudden, loud, creaking sound. The drawbridge was coming down.

"They made it!" cried Tag.

Realizing that the cats would escape, the dogs rushed them, even without the general's orders. The cats formed a semi-circle and tried to defend their position. They were nearly overwhelmed by so many attackers. Mandy raced over and defended Brian from a dog that managed to get behind him. Softy feverishly continued to keep the dogs off balance by tripping them, but there were just too many. The other cats who had been rescued from the dungeon also did their best.

"We can't hold out much longer!" cried April, who blocked a strong dog's attack with difficulty.

Tag glanced quickly at the forest treetops coming into view behind him. "Once it's open...get ready to run!" he alerted the cats.

"What about the others?" Johnny replied as the semi-circle grew smaller and smaller.

"I don't know...," Tag responded, trying to focus on the two dogs attacking him.

Guarddog could see that the two cats were having trouble with the four attackers. "Switch with me," he told Mary as he left the wheel and joined them.

With Guarddog opposing them, the four dogs were stopped from advancing any further. Mary went to the wheel and immediately began turning it with all her strength.

Meanwhile, Licorice was fighting courageously. Whatever happened, he had decided, they had to get that drawbridge down and give the others enough time to escape. He blocked the attack of one dog and then powerfully struck the sword of another, almost knocking it away from him. Then he attacked the first dog again.

Mary and Harie cranked the wheels as quickly as they could, and the end of the drawbridge gradually descended. Licorice and Guarddog valiantly defended them from the four attacking dogs.

"How are *we* going to get out of here?" Mary dared to ask the others in the middle of all that was going on. There were already four soldiers in the area with them, and more were sure to come.

"I was hoping someone *else* would think of *that*," Guarddog replied, entirely occupied with his current task. Harie offered no response, and he looked rather concerned.

Mary was quite alarmed; *neither* the dog *nor* the rabbit knew how they were supposed to escape. She surveyed the area, trying to think.

"Through the holes where the chains are!" she declared. "We should be able to fit." She looked at the holes nervously. It seemed like a dangerous plan, but it was better than nothing.

"I knew you'd think of something," Harie told her warmly.

Mary and Harie continued turning the wheels, but it was taking too long. The drawbridge was only halfway down, and they could see King Wolf himself with a group of at least ten soldiers approaching from the end of the upper walkway. Harie stared at the large lever in front of him, desperate for anything that would allow them to lower the drawbridge faster.

"What does this lever do?" he called to Guarddog.

"Nothing!" Guarddog replied with frustration. "It just releases the gears for raising the drawbridge."

Harie and Mary just looked at each other. "*Releases* them?" they both said together.

Harie gave the big lever a tug, and with a rusty screech of metal against metal, the mechanism that had been keeping the drawbridge from falling under its own weight was disconnected. A loud whine was emitted as the wheels began to spin out of control and the chains were let out. The drawbridge went crashing to the ground with a loud wham. At the same time, King Wolf and his group of soldiers had just arrived.

"Go now!" Guarddog urged Mary and Harie.

Immediately the two of them were scrambling through the openings in the wall, which were just big enough for a cat, rabbit, or medium-sized dog to fit through. They emerged on the outside of the castle, hanging from the chains above the castle's entryway.

As additional soldiers arrived, Licorice and Guarddog each went to one of the holes. Licorice, with the guards surrounding him, ducked down and threw himself in, dropping his sword as it collided with the wall.

At the same time, Guarddog made a wide swing with his sword, brushing back the four nearest dogs. Briefly forgetting his fear of heights, he then dove into the opening and squirmed his way through. The dogs' swords clattered harmlessly on the wall behind him.

King Wolf had caught sight of Licorice before he dove into the opening. "Raise the drawbridge!" ordered the king. "I want that cat!"

A pair of dogs immediately seized the two wheels and started turning them back in the other direction.

Once the drawbridge hit ground, the cats below turned and raced across it. Before all of them even reached the end, though, it started rising up again. Some of the cats had to leap across a small part of the moat. Ben, one of the last ones, slipped at the end of the bridge and toppled into the dark water. Several dogs also jumped across to continue the battle, while the general was stuck inside the castle.

A number of cats found themselves still under attack. Whitey charged one dog and pushed him into the moat. Johnny was knocked down from behind by another, but he managed to trip the dog and get back to his feet. With his extra-long fur dripping with muddy water, Ben fiercely reared up out of the moat with his sword raised and faced a dog that was smaller than him—the dog yelped and then ran away squealing. Ben looked over at Richard and shrugged his shoulders, not understanding why the dog had been scared.

Though the cats wanted to flee, they knew they had to wait for their friends. How those four would escape, no one knew, but if they didn't come soon…April was the first to spot them hanging from the chains above the rising drawbridge.

"There they are!" she called out, pointing.

Up above, Harie, Mary, Licorice, and Guarddog each climbed as quickly as they could, paw after paw, down the chains. Unfortunately, the chains were working against them, moving them back up toward the castle wall.

The king watched from the window to see how much progress they were making. "Turn it faster!" he sharply ordered his soldiers.

Harie was the first to reach the end of the drawbridge. Being a good jumper, he immediately sprang across to the other side of the moat.

Mary reached the end of the chain and turned to wait for Licorice, who was not far behind her. Licorice finally caught up, and together they glanced fearfully downward at the mass of dogs blocked in below by the inclined drawbridge. By now, they were too high up to jump safely onto the land, but Licorice was keenly aware of the alligators who resided down below in the moat. Mary, however, was not thinking about the gators—before Licorice knew it, she was reaching around his waist and leaning both of their bodies out toward the water.

"No, wait! We can't..." Licorice protested.

Mary realized his meaning just as they lost their balance. As they tipped over the edge, she instinctively reached out and grabbed him around the neck while somehow still holding her sword in her other paw. At the same time, Licorice turned and caught the end of the bridge with his forepaws. The two of them hung precariously above the water as the drawbridge continued to rise. Licorice glanced downward and saw the gators positioning themselves beneath them.

Guarddog's view of Licorice and Mary was blocked by the immense bridge. From his location, still too far up on the chain, it looked as though they had jumped into the moat. Knowing that he could never do *that*, he watched as the castle wall drew nearer. He resigned himself to being taken into custody and to receive whatever punishment King Wolf would exact upon him.

King Wolf had taken his eyes off the drawbridge for only a second to observe his soldiers turning the wheels. When he turned back, his eyes opened wide with rage and disbelief as the cats appeared to be gone. Since Licorice was the one he wanted, he gave his soldiers a new order. "Release the drawbridge!"

Guarddog heard the order from outside the window— completely astounded, he held on tightly...At once, the soldiers all stepped back and let go of the wheels.

Licorice and Mary felt the drawbridge give way and suddenly found themselves falling. Licorice pushed them both clear from the bridge just before it smashed into the ground, and they both tumbled roughly but safely in the dirt.

As the drawbridge hit, Guarddog was jarred loose from the chain but used the momentum to propel himself onto the shore. As he rolled to his feet, he saw the swarm of soldiers from within the castle stampeding towards him. Several of them threw their spears—the savvy fighter tucked in his head and blocked one with his sword.

"Let's go!" he shouted as he, Licorice, and Mary ran away from the castle and the mob of dogs.

Now that the cats knew everyone was outside, they stopped battling and turned to flee into the forest.

For the first few minutes, it was a dogged chase. The dogs could see their quarry just within reach, and they were determined not to let them get away. Before long, though, the cats' will for freedom gave them the extra energy needed to outrun their pursuers. Eventually they became untraceable amongst the trees, and the dogs had no choice but to concede their escape.

Since the king knew the cats were too far out of reach, he instructed the rest of his troops not to bother following them. Although his prisoners had gotten away, he still had the information he needed.

XVI
The Mountain

The animals raced through the forest, unsure of whether they were still being pursued or not. One by one, they hurdled over logs and brushed past bushes and branches.

Licorice was somewhere in the middle of the pack. He could see Tag running up ahead of him, trying to lead the way, with Softy hanging on tightly. "Tag! Wait!" he called out. "We can't go that way!"

Several of the animals including Tag knew what Licorice was talking about, and they helped stop the others. The entire group gathered by a giant, fallen tree. They all listened carefully but could not hear anybody approaching them. As Guarddog had reminded him back in the castle, Licorice knew they could not go home yet.

"Okay," Tag said to him first. "You say you found the crystal?"

Licorice was ashamed of what had happened, but he knew there wasn't much time. It was difficult to explain, but he had to try.

"I found it when they took us out in the search party—well, almost. The guards caught me before I could get to it, but now they know where it is. We have to get to it before King Wolf does!"

Tag looked at him uncertainly. "If you didn't get to it, then how could you have found it?" he asked logically.

"I could *sense* it," answered Licorice. "It was attracting me to it. I was trying to climb the mountain to escape from the guards, but then I realized that wasn't the reason at all. It was because the crystal was there."

Tag could tell that his brother believed in what he was saying, but Licorice had been acting recklessly ever since Mary had been captured. Now he wanted them all to climb some mountain because he thought he had found the crystal—when he hadn't even seen it. It all seemed so unlikely—and yet...

"I was there," said Mary, supporting Licorice. "The king *said* Licorice knows where the crystal is."

The others began to debate the issue, but Tag had stopped listening. He didn't *want* to be related to the cat who had hidden the crystal. If he were drawn further into this conflict amongst the animals—which had started before he was even born—he didn't know if he had the strength to do all that would be required of him. They were lucky to have made it his far—to have rescued everyone and escaped from Dog Castle.

He couldn't deny, though, that what Licorice had told them *would* fit with everything they had heard about the crystal. It would certainly explain why, out of all the cats in Suburb City, *he* had been the one to organize an expedition to the Animals' Forest—in spite of his determination to stay away from there.

"I think we have to see for ourselves," Johnny was saying to him. "It's the only way to know for sure."

Some of the others nodded in agreement.

"And it makes sense," Guarddog added. "All the other cats were captured from the town, but Licorice was the only one who came to the Forest on his own. That's why he's here, and if you're his brother, that's why *you're here*."

Tag knew they were right. He didn't know what relative of his could have hidden the crystal, but if his brother said it was at the top of some mountain, then he had to trust him. If King Wolf knew about it, then they had to get there first. He sighed heavily.

"Okay," he agreed. "Which way do we go?"

Licorice was surprised at first. He had feared that Tag and the others wouldn't believe him. Instead, his story seemed to make perfect sense to them, especially with Mary and Guarddog's help explaining it. He felt better now that he had the others' support—and a more profound understanding of his previous, impulsive actions.

"That way," he said, pointing to the highest peak of the nearby mountains.

The group was complemented now by seven of the prisoner-cats who had also escaped across the drawbridge. These cats were grateful for being rescued and determined to help find the crystal. Two of the prisoners who had escaped with them had gotten separated from the group, but there was no time to go looking for them. Hopefully they would make it back to the town on their own.

The group was in a hurry, so the animals started off by jogging, but after a while they slowed down to walk. They were already quite exhausted from their efforts that morning, and there was no way they could run the whole distance. As the group moved along, the mountain gradually grew larger in front of them.

Eventually the landscape started sloping upward, and the animals knew they had reached the foot of the mountain. Wearily, they started trekking uphill, trying to take the easiest path to the top.

Most of the time, they could just walk. Only in a few places did they have to do much climbing. The steep hillside tired the group even more, but they knew they had to beat the Canine Order to the top, so they kept going. Softy rode on Tag's shoulder, as there was no other way he could keep up.

As the group progressed further, Licorice began to get the same excited feeling he had experienced before when he was here, and it gave him extra energy to push ahead. Tag, to his surprise, felt something, too. He couldn't explain it, but he now understood what Licorice had meant before. He knew somehow that he was related to the cat who had hidden the crystal, and he felt strangely compelled to reach the top of the mountain. Johnny, too, felt energized by being on the mountain. He knew he couldn't be related to the cat who had found the crystal if Tag and Licorice were, but for some reason, he felt as if he could sense the crystal as well.

The air became cooler as the group climbed higher. The mountain was densely lined with trees near the bottom, but as the animals forged on, the amount of plant life began to decrease. The group was moving very slowly now, but they could only hope that the Canine Order would not be any faster.

After a while, there were hardly any trees around at all. The area became mostly rocky. Just when the animals thought they might be near the top, another ridge would come into view.

Finally, after one last exhausting hour, the animals reached a plateau. Tag, Licorice, Johnny, and Softy eagerly ran out onto the large, open area, hoping to see the crystal.

At first they were uncertain. There seemed to be nothing there. As the rest of the group emerged from below, though, the three cats realized where they needed to go. Up ahead, across a deep gorge, was the mountain's summit.

The three cats raced to the ledge and overlooked the giant chasm. It was ten yards across—and a long way down. Now everyone approached the gorge. It was rather breezy up on the plateau.

"We need to get to the other side," Licorice stated with certainty.

Tag and Johnny knew he was right; they all looked around for something that would help them cross the ravine.

Johnny spotted a scraggly, dead tree, the only one nearby. "We can use that," he said, pointing.

The group approached the tree, and several of them pushed on it. The tree started to tilt, and its dirt-covered roots began to emerge from the ground. Eventually the whole thing toppled over. It looked like it would be long enough.

Several of the cats snapped off the brittle roots and branches so the tree would be easier to walk on. They chopped at the thicker ones with their swords until they could remove them.

The tree was fairly light, easy for the cats to pick up. They carried it over to the gorge. There, with a little direction from Johnny and Brian, the group raised the tree onto its end, gave it a shove in the right direction, and tried to hold onto the base as it fell across. The other end of the tree smashed into the ground on the other side and bounced slightly before coming to rest.

"Let's go," Johnny said, feeling extremely anxious.

"Not everyone," Tag pointed out. "It's going to be risky crossing to the other side, and we don't need everyone just to get the crystal."

"I'll go," said Licorice. "I'll be able to find it."

"We'll both go," said Tag, to show his brother that he, too, could sense the nearness of the crystal.

"Well, I want to go, too," said Johnny. Oddly, he had the strangest feeling that it was *he* who should be going.

Tag understood that Johnny wanted to stick with him and Licorice all the way to the top, but it just wasn't worth the extra risk. "Licorice and I are the only ones who should go," he said once again, putting his paw on his friend's shoulder. "Don't worry—we'll be back before long."

"I guess…," Johnny reluctantly agreed. "Well, be careful," he told them.

The rest of the group expressed the same sentiments.

Guarddog looked over the edge and started to feel dizzy. He backed away faintly. "I think I'll stay here," he muttered to Harie.

It would be easier to balance without carrying anything, so Tag handed his sword and shoulder harness to Guarddog. Licorice had already lost his sword above Dog Castle's drawbridge. They both turned to face the narrow log.

Tag set his paw on the makeshift overpass and tried to shake it. Unfortunately, since the log was so light, it shifted easily from side to side in the dirt near the cats.

Johnny looked at his friends with concern. "We'll hold it steady for you," he decided. He, Mandy, Mary, and April knelt near the log so they could brace it.

Tag nodded with appreciation. "We'd better go one at a time," he said to Licorice.

"Okay," Licorice agreed. "I'll go first."

Licorice stepped up onto the wooden walkway. It was just wide enough for him to stand with his hind legs about shoulder-width apart and his ankles angled slightly downward along the curvature of the log. With his knees bent and forearms spread out to the side, he began inching his way out over the chasm. With each step, it seemed as if the log might slide right out from underneath him. Gradually, though, he worked his way across to the other side. He leaped back onto solid ground and looked back anxiously, barely able to wait for his brother before continuing onward.

Then it was Tag's turn. He gingerly stepped onto the wobbly log. Step by step, he treaded out over the abyss. As he reached the middle, though, he suddenly slipped on some dirt and was thrown off balance! His hind legs slid out to the side and he dropped down, catching the log jarringly with his forearms. The whole group held their breath as Tag dangled precariously above the chasm.

From both ends of the log, Licorice and Johnny got ready to go help him, but with great difficulty, Tag gathered his strength and started to pull himself up. He swung his lower body side to side to get some momentum and then hoisted one of his rear paws up on top of the log. Then he proceeded to pull his whole body back on top. He was facing the wrong way, back toward the plateau, but at least he was still in one piece. He stayed low on the log and backed his way to the side where Licorice waited.

"Next time, be more careful," Licorice wryly advised him as he stepped down from the log.

"I *was* being careful," Tag responded, staring intently down into the gorge.

"Let's go," Licorice urged his brother, drawing him away from the ledge.

Looking back across the way, the two brothers waved to their friends to show that they were okay. Then they turned toward the mountain's summit. A winding path with scattered patches of snow led to the top.

XVII
The Caretaker

Tag and Licorice marched confidently up the steep slope. The ground was cold, and a brisk wind was blowing. With every step, they could feel themselves getting closer to the crystal.

The two brothers could no longer see their friends. As they moved along the narrow path, walls of rock obscured their view. After another thirty minutes or so, they could see the highest point of the mountain. They knew the crystal had to be there.

As Tag and Licorice approached the peak, they noticed a large bird's nest situated amongst the rocks there. Before they could get to it, though, the path became quite steep and they were forced to climb. The last part before the nest became nearly flat again.

The two cats walked up to the nest. There was nowhere else for the crystal to be.

From here, Tag and Licorice could see the entire Animals' Forest around them. The lush, green forest, which had never been affected by people, stretched all the way to massive mountains that were considerably taller than this one. In one direction they could see all the way to the city. Suddenly, a large bird poked its head up from within the deep nest, startling the two cats.

"What do you want?" it demanded in an agitated voice. Its neck and face were featherless, and its skin was of a light red color. It was a giant condor!

Tag and Licorice were surprised to have encountered an animal in such an unlikely place, and they were somewhat unsettled from being caught off-guard. They looked at each other uncertainly.

"Um, we were wondering…," responded Tag as a chilly breeze whipped by, "have you seen a crystal around here?"

"A *what?*" the bird replied. "A *crystal?* Don't be ridiculous."

The condor sat up within the nest, and the two cats could see his upper body. He had long, beautiful, black feathers, with some white ones near the top of his chest.

Tag and Licorice were skeptical of the bird's response. They could sense that the crystal was near, and the condor seemed a bit defensive—like he was hiding something.

"You're sitting on it, aren't you?" Licorice challenged the magnificent-looking bird.

The condor appeared offended. "Why, I…how dare you accuse me of lying! I don't know what you're talking about."

"Yes you do," Licorice responded impatiently.

"No I don't…," the condor replied coolly.

"Yes you do!" argued Licorice, raising his voice.

"*No I do-on't,*" the condor sang back childishly.

Tag and Licorice looked at each other again. They didn't have time for games. The Canine Order could be there any minute, and they both knew the condor had the crystal.

"Listen," said Tag. "Have you heard of King Wolf? He lives in this forest."

"I know of King Wolf," the condor answered evenly.

"Well, he's on his way here," Tag informed the stubborn bird. "And he wants the crystal. He'll stop at nothing to take it from you."

"Crystal, crystal…I told you I have no crystal! If you don't believe me, why don't you just push me out of my nest and see for yourselves?"

The two cats could not help but to consider the idea. If they rushed the large bird, they could push him away, make him fly off, and at least see for a moment what was in the nest. They could even grab the crystal, if it was there, and run with it…Both cats knew, though, that it wasn't the right thing to do. If they were violent toward the bird, they would be no better than King Wolf.

Licorice, especially, remembered how awful he had felt after starting to fight with the bully, Toger, three days ago. He turned aside and spoke softly to Tag. "We can't do that," he said, "—we need to convince him somehow."

Tag nodded in agreement, with a certain approach in mind. "Let me try something," he whispered back.

The two cats faced the nest again.

"We won't push you," Tag told the obstinate condor. "But we know you have the crystal. If you don't give it to *us*, King Wolf's going to get it. You don't want *that*, do you?"

The shrewd bird looked at them sharply. "Several years ago," he began, "a cat named Julius climbed this mountain and came to my nest. He had the crystal of which you speak, and he told me all about it...about Wolf...the whole story. I told him I'd keep it for him and promised I wouldn't give it to *anyone*."

Tag and Licorice looked at each other with satisfaction—at least now they knew they were in the right place.

"Well—why didn't you say so?" questioned Licorice.

"Because I was testing you," the bird said matter-of-factly.

"*Testing* us?" repeated Licorice in disbelief.

"I had to make sure you weren't agents of King Wolf," the condor explained. "Surely you didn't think I could trust you just because you're cats."

"So then you'll give it to us," presumed Tag.

"No, I won't!" responded the condor. "I won't give it to anyone."

"But—" Tag began.

"Don't worry," the feathered creature assured them. "If King Wolf comes, I'll take it in my talons and fly away. He'll never be able to catch me. You needn't worry. The crystal is perfectly safe with me. I'm afraid you came up here for nothing."

Tag and Licorice hadn't thought of *that*. They stepped aside to discuss the matter.

"I guess," said Tag, "that he can protect the crystal better than we can."

"Yeah," Licorice agreed. "How could the Canine Order catch him if he can fly away?"

"So...I guess we can go now," concluded Tag.

"I guess so," agreed Licorice.

To both cats, it seemed a bit disappointing to leave with nothing to show for their trouble, but no one could have known that the crystal would be in the custody of a living, breathing caretaker. The cat who had "hidden" the crystal had been very clever indeed. The two brothers turned back toward the condor.

"We'll be going then," Tag told the bird.

"Sorry to disturb you," added Licorice.

"That's okay," replied the condor. "I don't get much company up here anyways."

The two cats laughed at the bird's reply. Still feeling a bit uncertain, they turned and started to head back down the path. Just as they were about to go down the steep part, though, the condor called out to them.

"Wait! Come back! I have to tell you something!"

Tag and Licorice turned and hiked back up to the nest. They looked at the condor questioningly.

"The fact is," said the condor, "the crystal is too slippery for me to hold onto. Its sides are hard and smooth, and if I carry it very far, it slips out of my talons. If King Wolf comes, I'm afraid there's not much I can do to protect it from him."

The two cats were confounded—one minute the bird wouldn't admit he had the crystal, and the next he was saying he could keep it safe, when really he couldn't.

"Then why did you say you could?" asked Tag with bewilderment.

The condor adjusted his position within the nest before answering. "I was still testing you," explained the unpredictable bird. "I had to make sure of your intentions. I knew one day a relative of Julius would come for the crystal, but I had no way to tell who it was—just that he or she would be a cat. You still could have been King Wolf's agents, or maybe you just wanted the crystal for yourselves...But the crystal gave me a vision. It showed me that only if an animal were telling the truth, and only if he or she were worthy of it, would he or she be willing to leave *without* it."

Tag and Licorice remembered what the old cat had told them about the crystal's power to give glimpses into the future, so the condor's account made sense to them. They realized now that the bird was, in fact, going to give them the crystal, but at the same time—for the first time—they felt a bit uncertain about taking it.

"But what if we're *not* really worthy of it?" questioned Licorice, who knew he had made some mistakes and had not always done the right thing. "We just know we're related to the cat who hid it, and no one ever knew why *he* was always attracted back to it."

"I don't know," said the condor. "All I know is that I've had the crystal with me for a long time, and I've gained a *few* bits of knowledge from it. The Animals' Forest is a place for animals to live in peace and to develop their own society, and the crystal is a tool to help them do so. But while a forest can attract many animals, one crystal can only attract one animal—or a few. So the crystal linked itself with the first animal who was decent and who would not exploit its powers for selfish reasons. Julius wasn't the purest of heart, nor was he the only one it could have been—but he was the first one who was good *enough* and who came close enough to find it. Now, you're his relatives and you're here…That means it's *your* turn to take care of it."

Tag and Licorice were speechless for a moment as the importance—and the difficulty—of such a responsibility started to sink in.

"So then King Wolf can never really *keep* the crystal," reasoned Tag.

"That's right," said the condor. "It will always come back to your family—eventually. But anyone can *use* it. So guard the crystal with your lives. If King Wolf gets it, many animals will suffer his wrath before it does."

The condor hopped up onto the edge of the nest. "Here," he said. "Take it, and have a safe journey."

At the bottom of the nest lay the crystal. It was about seven inches in diameter, imperfectly symmetric, with numerous smooth sides that formed a complex but aesthetically pleasing pattern. It was transparent and mostly colorless, except for a faint hint of pink. Though its appearance was attractive to the eye, there was no outward indication of the power it actually exuded.

Tag and Licorice were quite overwhelmed by all they had just learned, but they both realized that they really had no choice at this point. No matter what reason they were there, or who was related to whom, they still needed to move the crystal to safety before King Wolf got it.

Licorice climbed up over the edge of the nest and scooped up the crystal with two paws. He held it out for Tag to touch, and immediately the two cats truly understood what the old cat at the Cougar Club Coffee Shop had been talking about. Even though they had never seen or touched the crystal before, it was familiar to them, as if they had.

Just as Tag was about to remove his paw from the crystal, though, an image popped into his head. He and Licorice were back on the log spanning the gorge, yet the log was falling! He could see the log disappearing from his sight below him and he felt weightless. At the same time, he could feel himself reaching desperately for the cliff, and he could see Licorice doing the same—then the image was gone. He was still standing at the condor's nest near the mountain peak as his paw slipped off the crystal.

Tag wasn't exactly sure what had just happened. All he knew was that it wasn't real, yet it had been more than just his imagination. "Thanks," he said nervously to the condor, a little too shaken up to say anything more.

Licorice, who had not experienced anything unusual, wondered how to use the crystal, but he was in too much of a hurry to worry about it right now.

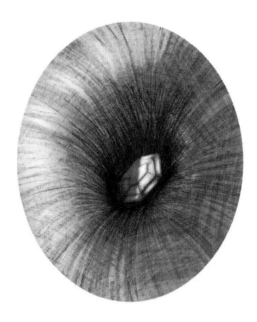

The condor could sense the cats' trepidation as they prepared to take the crystal with them, so he gave them one more piece of advice. "Remember, visions from the crystal originate from within *you*, so if your reasons for wanting the crystal are noble, trust those visions, and the crystal will always return to you."

The two brothers nodded in agreement, even though neither of them really understood how to interpret the advice. Tag's vision, in particular, only seemed to forecast their impending doom. The two brothers turned to go.

The cats made their way down the winding slope. For the moment, Tag was quite content to let Licorice carry the crystal. As they walked, though, he finally gathered himself enough to describe to his brother the eerie vision he had foreseen.

"When I touched the crystal, I saw a vision," he told Licorice.

"You did?" replied Licorice, feeling both curious and maybe a little jealous.

"I saw us on the log, but the log was falling and we were jumping," Tag said.

Licorice was a bit startled by the ominous prophecy. He was unsure of what to say at first, but then the next question seemed obvious.

"Did we make it?"

"I don't know," answered Tag. "I didn't see the end."

Neither of the two cats was thrilled now by the prospect of crossing the gorge once again, especially Tag, who had slipped the first time. Before long, though, the brothers arrived back at the ravine and the narrow log. They saw all their friends there, waiting anxiously on the other side. Licorice held up the crystal for everyone to see, and all their comrades let out a cheer. Tag and Licorice's spirits were lightened for the moment.

Then everyone heard a gruff voice call out from where they had come up the mountain.

"Hold it right there, you cats!"

It was the voice of King Wolf.

XVIII
The Battle on the Plateau

The group turned and looked out across the plateau. King Wolf was there, with a brigade of at least fifty dogs.

The king moved slowly and steadily towards them while his soldiers spread out, eagerly gripping the hilts of their swords. General Doverman was at the king's side.

"It was so nice of you to retrieve the crystal for us," the king bellowed. "Now, if you hand it over, we'll spare your lives, and there will be jobs for *all* of you in the new kingdom of animals under *my* authority."

It was clear to the cats that even after all these years, the king's thirst for power had not diminished. Though he had tried to make the offer sound reasonable, the cats knew that a job for them under the reign of Wolf meant a life of slavery. Their alternative, however, was a battle they couldn't possibly win.

"What should we do?" said Richard.

"Well, we can't surrender," said April.

"And we can't give them the crystal," said Mary. "If we do, everyone will be doomed."

"But we're outnumbered—and trapped," said Blackey.

"We can't give them the crystal," said Guarddog. "It's out of the question."

"Then we'll have to fight," determined Mandy.

It was a solemn moment as everyone in the group nodded in agreement. They all knew the consequences of their decision.

Seeing that everyone was in accord, Johnny stepped to the front of the group. He shared a quick glance of mutual understanding with Guarddog, then took a deep breath.

"Never!" he boldly called back to the king.

"Think carefully, you cats," the evil king warned. "You're not in a very good position."

"Everyone spread out," said Johnny. "And try to keep them from getting to the other side of the gorge."

The king watched as the animals took their positions a few yards apart from each other. "So be it!" he yelled. "Ready your weapons," he commanded his troops.

All the dogs drew their swords. Then the king gave the order.

"Ataaaaack!"

The dogs charged across the plateau with their swords raised above their heads.

As they approached, Guarddog realized a problem. "We need to get away from this cliff so we can have more room," he directed the others. Then he took off, dashing forward to meet the onrushing dogs. All the cats followed his lead, charging forward bravely.

The animals met their antagonists a little farther from the cliff, but not nearly enough. There were at least two dogs for every one of them. Two dogs even went after Softy, who had to dodge their swords.

"Get that mouse!" one of them shouted viciously.

Tag and Licorice watched the battle unfold. They knew their friends would not be able to keep it up for long.

"We have to help them," said Licorice, abruptly deciding to cross the log and get it over with. He started to move forward, but Tag held him back. At first, Licorice thought his brother was just scared to cross, but then he realized what he saw.

"It's too late," Tag muttered, looking across the chasm.

A handful of dogs, led by King Wolf, had easily broken through and was heading straight for them. In a matter of seconds, the group had reached the edge of the gorge only ten yards away. Two dogs knelt down to hold the log steady, and the rest started coming across.

Johnny attacked the nearest dog with a swift movement. The dog blocked it and responded with a series of blows toward all parts of his body. Johnny proficiently blocked every move and then turned to face the next dog. That dog was holding his sword over his head, and he swung down at Johnny. Johnny held his sword up to block and then turned it in a circular motion, removing the dog's sword from his grip and flinging it several yards away. A third dog came at him, but he stepped aside and pushed the dog away.

Meanwhile, Ben charged fearlessly at two opposing dogs. With two strong moves, he knocked both of their swords away from them. Just as he relaxed, however, another dog came up behind him, and he barely had time to turn and block. Unfortunately, the dog had lunged forward out of control and ended up landing on top of him. Ben struggled and pushed with all his might to get the dog's sword out of the way. Slowly, he managed to push the sword slightly up, just enough to roll out to the side. He leaped to his feet just in time to face the first two dogs again.

One dog attacked Mandy with four different moves. Skillfully using her sword, she blocked them all firmly and parried a thrust made by another dog. The first dog attacked again. Mandy blocked it and attacked; the dog blocked it and swung for her legs. Mandy jumped to avoid it. The second dog swung for her neck, but she ducked and then attacked the dog's torso. The dog defended himself and then continued his attack. Mandy continued to defend herself.

Blackey was busy trying to look after Whitey and defend himself at the same time. Whitey charged madly at a pair of dogs and swung his sword. The two dogs ducked and both swung back at Whitey. Whitey managed to block both of them, but then a third dog came at him from behind. Knowing that Whitey didn't see the third dog, Blackey turned and tackled the oncoming attacker. Just as he landed, though, the dog he had been facing prepared to strike him. Whitey turned and blocked the attack, saving his brother.

"Thanks," said Blackey as he got up. The two of them moved away readily, trying to watch each other's back.

April was occupied by another pair of ferocious dogs. She would pretend to run away and then turn back and attack. This cunning tactic kept the dogs confused as they tried to pursue her.

At the same time, Richard was in trouble. He started out by having his sword knocked out of his paws. He dodged one of the dogs' blows, tripped, and fell. He swiftly rolled over, grabbed his sword, and took a wild swing at the legs of one of the dogs. The dog leaped back out of the way, giving Richard time to get back on his feet and block an attack from another dog.

Guarddog used his two swords to battle three opponents. The skilled warrior blocked an upper and a lower attack from two of the dogs at the same time. Then he blocked the third dog and one of the first two. Spinning around, he blocked the first dog with one sword and attacked with the other. That dog barely blocked it and swung for his legs, but Guarddog jumped into the air and did a flip. He came down with a powerful, majestic blow towards the dog's shoulder. The dog was able to block it but fell over as a result. The skilled warrior turned and simultaneously attacked the other two.

One dog immediately knocked Mary's sword away from her, sending it flying several yards away. Again the dog attacked, but Mary desperately leaped to her side, both to avoid the move and to get closer to her sword. As the dog approached, she rose up into a squatting position. When the dog swung at her mid-section, she sprang as far as she could into a somersault, almost to her sword. As the dog rushed over towards her, she surged forward and grabbed the sword. Kneeling, she turned and managed to block the dog's next attack. She then rose to her feet and continued to fight, blocking that dog and another two who came at her from behind.

At that very moment, a pair of dogs was charging at Brian. At first he began to retreat, but the dogs kept coming, so he had no choice but to hold his ground. As soon as Brian came to a stop, the two attackers swung their swords at the same time. Brian leaped into the air, avoiding the attack to his legs and simultaneously using his sword to block the move for his chest. When he landed, he swung at one dog, then the other, but both blocked him easily.

The first dog lunged at Brian with his sword pointing straight forward, but Brian handily stepped to the side and tripped him while blocking the sword. The dog dropped his sword as he hit the ground and tried to reach for it, but Brian kicked the sword away from him. The dog went scurrying after it while Brian concentrated on the second dog and got ready for a third attacker approaching from the side.

Harie was stuck battling a pair of exceptionally strong opponents. Every time he blocked their attacks he was forced backwards, and soon he found that his back was to the cliff. As one of the dogs swung again, Harie dove to his left. Though he was not too close to the cliff anymore, the dog was upon him instantly. The dog raised his sword and thrust it straight down, but Harie rolled to his side and avoided it. He barely had time to scramble to his feet before the other dog lunged at him, this time with a series of movements. Harie blocked a few but resorted to dodging since blocking was quite difficult.

During this time, Softy raced from dog to dog, trying to trip them and keep them off balance. A pair of dogs followed him and swatted at him with their swords. Softy scurried back and forth, constantly eluding them, but the dogs kept after him with deadly determination.

The other seven cats fought valiantly as well, but the brave animals knew they were fighting a losing battle. King Wolf and his soldiers had already broken past them to get to Tag, Licorice, and the crystal. Now the cats were purely on the defensive, running about the plateau, trying to keep their opponents at bay and to assist each other when they could. There was no way they could help Tag and Licorice, nor was there any way to escape.

The dogs seemed very adept at crossing the log, perhaps from all their training. Tag and Licorice knew they could push the log into the ravine, but then they would be trapped with no way to help their friends.

Before long, the first few dogs had made it all the way across. The two cats knew they couldn't stop them, especially with no weapons. Instinctively they backed away, moving downhill along the sloping hillside.

Soon King Wolf stepped off of the log. Along with six of his soldiers, he advanced toward the two cats. Tag and Licorice continued backing up until their backs were to a cliff. The dogs were only a few yards away now.

"Now, you cats," demanded the king over the sound of the harsh wind, "hand over the crystal."

XIX
The Cats and the Crystal

Tag answered back to the king. "If you come any closer, we'll throw the crystal away!"

Licorice was surprised at first by Tag's threat, but he knew his brother was right. Even if they couldn't escape, they still mustn't let the king get his paws on the crystal. To show that he would do it, he held out the crystal towards the valley below.

"Go ahead!" the king roared. "We'll just climb down there and get it later, after we finish you off!"

Tag looked at Licorice despairingly. The king was right; even if they did drop the crystal, it would only delay him from getting it—it would not stop him.

"Nice try," Licorice told Tag, withdrawing the crystal and clutching it tightly to his chest. Then suddenly *he* had a vision! He saw the crystal itself soaring straight upward into the sky…and that was all…

Licorice shook his head, a bit dazed by the experience just as Tag had been. He wished his brother had seen it, too, but he knew it had to mean something. "I just saw something," he whispered as the dogs moved closer. "I saw the crystal flying up in the air."

Tag understood that Licorice meant a vision from the crystal, just as he had seen. He was baffled at first, but he tried to think. "The condor said the crystal would always return to us...," he contemplated.

Just then, from somewhere behind them, they both heard a piercing screech from what sounded like a bird of prey. Glancing back quickly, they both noticed the condor up in the sky, urgently swooping towards them.

Tag and Licorice were nearing the same conclusion at about the same time. The dogs were only a few feet away now.

"So we should..."

"Throw it, Licorice!"

The king realized what he was doing only as Licorice bent his knees and held the crystal down low. The dogs watched in disbelief as he sent it arcing high up into the air above everyone.

At the same time, the condor flapped his wings to increase his speed. Tag and Licorice watched frightfully as the crystal reached its apex and started to fall—right toward King Wolf.

The king's eyes stayed fixed on the crystal and he licked his chops eagerly. Just as he was about to catch it, though, the condor snatched it out of the air with his talons.

With his wings fully extended, the majestic creature was about ten feet wide. Instead of appearing graceful, though, the condor bobbed up and down clumsily in the air, trying to secure the slippery object in his grasp. The two cats were astonished that he had caught it at all, considering what he'd told them. Indeed, it looked like he would drop it any second.

Though it was hard for anyone to take their eyes off the otherwise magnificent-looking bird soaring through the air with the prize they sought, Tag had the presence of mind to pull Licorice forward. The two cats daringly darted between the distracted dogs. Each of the two cats seized a dog's sword as he went by.

The king was infuriated. "Get that crystal!" he ordered his troops, but the condor, who still did not have a firm grip on the object, had already drifted out over the ravine. The dogs saw the two cats heading for the log and followed them instead.

Just as the condor cleared the gorge, he bobbled the crystal, and it fell from the sky—right toward Johnny!

Johnny was battling a dog near the cliff when a ten-foot shadow passed over him. He glanced upwards just in time to see the crystal coming at him, and amazingly he was able to catch it with both paws. Just as he did, however, the dog he was facing rushed at him.

Johnny deftly stepped to the side and pushed the dog, sending him stumbling out-of-control toward the precipice. It all happened so fast that by the time Johnny looked in that direction, he could only hear the dog's mournful voice calling from somewhere nearby, out of sight.

"Help! Heeelp!"

Stepping over to the cliff, Johnny found his adversary dangling from a narrow ledge. Then, as he held the crystal, he suddenly had a realization. *He, too,* was related to the cat who had hidden it! How it could be possible, he didn't know, but there was no doubt that it was true. He had been sensing it for some time now but had been denying it to himself. Now, with the crystal in his possession, the truth was much too strong to ignore.

Guarddog was nearby, occupied by two opponents, and he had seen what had occurred. The dog Johnny had pushed was Clarence, whom he had encountered back in Dog Castle's courtyard. "Johnny!" he called. "Save that dog! He's my friend!"

"Please! Help!" the dog cried pitifully, looking up at Johnny.

Johnny looked back at Guarddog with confusion. They were in the middle of a battle, and this dog had just attacked him.

"It's okay," Guarddog assured him. "You can trust him."

Surprised by the request, Guarddog's two opponents briefly refrained from their assault to see what Johnny would do. Just as Guarddog relaxed, however, he was caught off guard by a third attacker. That dog swung at him strongly, and although Guarddog managed to block the strike, one of his swords was knocked to the ground. He stumbled to his side and, with his remaining sword, barely fended off the next few moves. His new opponent was General Doverman.

Johnny wasn't sure whether to listen to Guarddog or not. Although the dog had been vital to their escape from Dog Castle, Johnny still did not know him that well. Could he trust his judgment on this matter? Saving the fallen dog was a terrible risk. Would the dog attack him again? Would he try to take the crystal from him?

As he knelt there, though, with the crystal in one paw, Johnny knew it was the chance he had to take. Since his first encounter with the Canine Order, he had learned to use his anger to overcome his fear and to make himself strong; but now, if he and his friends were deserving of the crystal and its power, they had to be brave enough to rise above their fears *and* their anger. After hearing Guarddog's plea, he couldn't just let the dog fall to his death.

Johnny set the crystal down and reached out his paw to the terrified dog. The dog desperately took hold and Johnny labored to pull him up.

It was just then that General Doverman noticed the crystal that Johnny had placed on the ground. Abruptly, he broke away from his struggle with Guarddog and tried to run towards it. Guarddog ran and tackled him, grabbing him around his hind legs.

With one final tug, the fallen dog was pulled to safety. Johnny looked at the dog, wondering if he'd just made a big mistake. The dog appeared uncertain of what he should do next.

"Kill him!" the general commanded him, still restrained on the ground by Guarddog. "Get the crystal!"

"He just saved you, Clarence," Guarddog shouted to the dog.

Clarence still did not move.

"If you get that crystal, you'll be honored by King Wolf and all the other dogs," the general enticed him. "You'll be a hero!"

"He's not your enemy," Guarddog continued. "We've been serving King Wolf for a long time, but it's time to leave this army."

The general noticed that the other two dogs who had been battling Guarddog had not moved. "Don't just stand there," he ordered them. "Go get the crystal!"

Hesitating only briefly, one of the dogs started to charge toward Johnny. The other one, looking uncertain, followed tentatively. Still sitting on the ground, Johnny grasped his sword and tried to get ready for them; but it was Clarence who jumped up, rushed forward, and rammed the first dog with his shoulder, sending them both hurtling to the ground. As they got up, the attacker looked at Clarence with confusion, and the second dog stopped near the other two without attacking.

Then Johnny could see the three of them having a serious discussion. Clarence was gesturing frantically, and the others kept looking at Johnny, as well as Guarddog and the general. Johnny watched with bewilderment as the three dogs left both him and the general alone and headed out into the midst of the battle. At the moment, he couldn't even remember why he had saved the first dog.

With King Wolf and the other six dogs approaching, Tag and Licorice stepped onto the log. Although they were still worried about the vision Tag had described, they knew it was their only chance. If they could just get back to the plateau, they could push the log over the edge, leaving King Wolf stuck on the other side.

The king, realizing the same thing, called out to the two troops he had stationed near the log on the plateau. "Stop those cats! Don't let them off that log!"

Those two dogs heard the king and obeyed. Showing little regard for their own safety, they moved out onto the log toward the cats. Behind the two cats, a pair of dogs was starting out onto the log as well.

Tag and Licorice got to the middle before the two dogs were blocking Tag in front. Tag dug his hind claws into the tree bark and readied his sword, and Licorice did the same, facing the dogs behind them. They exchanged a quick, meaningful glance and prepared themselves. Below them was a thousand-foot drop.

Meanwhile, General Doverman had worked his way out of Guarddog's hold, and the two of them had resumed sword fighting. Fortunately, Guarddog had taken a position between the general and Johnny.

Johnny dared not go anywhere as long as he had the crystal with him. Instead, he watched the three dogs who had reentered the battlefield. They first interrupted the two dogs chasing Softy and spoke to them. Then the five of them split up and went in different directions. So far, no one else realized that Johnny had the crystal.

Mary was surprised when she found herself being assisted by a large dog. The same thing happened for Blackey and Whitey, who went on to help someone else. Gradually, a number of swordfights with the cats were being halted. Some of the dogs were talking to each other, and others were fighting each other

now. The tide of the battle was being turned, with some of the dogs going against their king.

"You have to force them back," Licorice urged Tag as he contended with the nearest dog.

"I'm trying!" Tag told him with frustration as he blocked a move that almost knocked him off balance. He swung back and, with a number of moves, drove the dogs back a few feet.

Licorice blocked a number of attacks by his opponent and then pushed him back. With more determination, that dog lunged at Licorice, almost knocking them *both* off the log. Licorice managed to push him back again.

At the same time, Tag was trying to be aggressive, to move the dogs back so they could get to solid ground. He carefully inched his hind paws forward on the log as he pressed his opponents back, and Licorice backed up with him. Eventually the cats were two thirds of the way there.

Unfortunately, the light log was shaking and rotating with every move the adversaries made. On the plateau side, it had shifted dangerously close to the edge.

Tag was the only one who could see the problem, and he couldn't help thinking that the vision he had seen was about to come true. "The log! It's slipping!" he direly tried to warn the dogs he was facing.

The dog nearest to him kept on attacking.

"I'm not lying!" Tag beseeched his foe. "We're all going to fall!"

The log shook abruptly, and everyone was thrown off balance. They all had to stop fighting and hold on with all four paws. As the dogs facing Tag stood up, they looked back and saw that it was true. There were only about six inches of the log left in contact with the plateau. If it slipped anymore, they would all be finished.

"Nobody move!" Tag implored all of them.

Everyone heard him and realized that he was right. They all stood still.

That was when Licorice realized something important—the dogs were just as scared of falling as they were. Then he remembered that the crystal's visions, as he had recently experienced, were not prophecies, but *ideas*. "Tag," he said pensively, "I think we *ought* to jump."

In an instant, Tag knew he was right. Just as the old storyteller cat had described, sometimes the crystal's visions didn't make sense until later. There had been no reason to jump from the log before, but now...

"We have to get these dogs out of the way," he said, half to himself. He knelt down and, with his forepaws, started to rock the log side to side, gently at first.

Licorice, who had barely heard him, realized what he was doing and started doing the same thing. The dogs on the log with them had no choice but to hold on.

Meanwhile, the king knew what was happening on the plateau and that he needed to get back there immediately. Only the two cats on the log were standing in his way—and his soldiers were not even fighting them.

"Get out of the way, you cowards!" he snapped, brushing aside two of his soldiers and storming onto the log even as it shook. He yanked the first dog back and flung him back to the ledge. The king showed tremendous balance—much better than any of his soldiers—as he marched forward on the moving log.

"We need to hurry!" shouted Licorice in alarm as the king came up behind the one remaining dog on his side. The two cats started rocking the log more strongly now.

The king struggled to maintain his balance but managed to grasp the second dog by his fur. Forcefully, he heaved that dog back toward the cliff, but the cliff was too far away—the dog flailed his limbs in futility and screamed as he fell out of sight into the gorge.

Now Tag and Licorice had seen first-hand just how cruel King Wolf could be. As the loathsome leader of the Canine Order came at Licorice with his sword wound up, ready to swing, the two cats shook the log as hard as they could.

"You fools!" shouted the king as he was forced to hold on with all four paws. "What are you doing, you crazy cats!?"

Then Tag used his front paws to try to pull the log *away* from the plateau.

The dogs opposing him, who were already holding on tightly, both looked back and saw that the log was nearly ready to slip from the edge. They turned and tried to get back to the plateau where they would be safe. King Wolf realized it, too, and had no choice but to withdraw from the log as well.

Tag and Licorice tried to follow the two dogs toward the plateau. As those two dogs made it to safety, though, the last one's paw kicked the last inch of the log away from the edge. The log lost its contact with the cliff and began to fall. The two brothers let go of their swords and desperately leaped with all their might...

They felt as if they were floating...The two cats barely reached the cliff with their front paws, and their bodies slammed into the rocks. Along with the cats' swords, the lightweight log plummeted into the ravine. It bounced off of a few ledges and then went sailing end over end into a freefall.

The two brothers pulled themselves up to safety. They looked out across the gorge and saw the king lying on the ground, angrily chewing out his soldiers. He, too, had jumped successfully from the log.

Suddenly, the dogs who had escaped the log with them had regained their composure. They charged toward the two cats, who were now unarmed. Before they could do anything, though, a number of dogs intercepted and battled them.

"What are you doing?!" cried one of the surprised soldiers.

Across the battlefield, there were about as many dogs *helping* the cats as fighting against them now. Several of the cats found themselves relieved from the battle. Clarence and another dog approached Guarddog and assisted him against General Doverman.

"Go on. Get out of here," Clarence told Guarddog.

"Thanks, my friend," said Guarddog, backing away. He understood that his friend wanted to repay him for convincing Johnny to save his life. He didn't know what would happen to Clarence or the others who had joined him, but he knew they would never rejoin the Canine Order.

"Traitors!" General Doverman cursed the other dogs. "You'll pay for this!"

Johnny watched as Clarence bravely took Guarddog's place. When he had saved the dog, he could not have imagined what would result. Could the crystal have influenced his decision? There was no way to know for sure.

Johnny and Guarddog raced across the battlefield, trying to round up all the cats plus Softy and Harie. Eventually Johnny met up with Tag and Licorice.

"Let's get going," he said anxiously.

"What happened?" questioned Licorice, relieved to find that his friend was okay—and holding the crystal.

"I caught the crystal," Johnny explained quickly, "—and then I saved a dog. Then he started to help us, and then some more did, and then—"

"Did you have a vision from the crystal?" Tag asked him.

Johnny gave him a funny look. "No," he answered. "Why?"

The three cats were about to run when they heard King Wolf yelling across the canyon.

"I'll get you cats! And the crystal—it will be mine!"

At the other end of the plateau, the three cats joined their friends and looked back across the open area. There were only dogs combating each other. General Doverman was busily barking out orders, trying to restore order, but it didn't seem to be making much difference. The king, meanwhile, was stranded on the other side of the ravine.

Tag and Licorice could see the condor circling high up in the sky overhead. They pointed him out to the others, and they all waved to him to thank him for his help. The condor saw them and dipped his wing, to say goodbye.

The group was eager to put some distance between themselves and the now-embattled Canine Order. They hastily headed down the mountain with the crystal safely in their possession.

XX
The Animals' Forest

The sun set as the group descended the mountain. As the animals made their way home in the dark, they happily recounted to each other their experiences on the plateau. Tag and Licorice described their encounter with the condor and how the crystal had provided them with visions that had helped them to save it and escape from King Wolf. Johnny and Guarddog explained how the battle had turned to their favor after the dog, Clarence, had been saved.

The animals passed the crystal around amongst themselves and soon discovered that its magic was not as easy to access as they had imagined. Most of them saw nothing, and for the few who did, the images were vague and difficult to understand. Guarddog had a vision of himself and Harie living in a community of many animals, dogs and cats alike, where he would be independent and have many friends. He took this notion to heart and decided to stick with Tag, Licorice, Johnny, and all the new friends he had made that day.

Johnny was still wondering how he could be related to the cat who had hidden the crystal when Tag and Licorice already seemed to be. He had a vision in which he saw himself encountering the old cat they had met a week ago in the alley. He decided to wait and ask him.

The animals were all overjoyed when at last they reached the outskirts of town. Despite their fatigue, they quickened their pace. They were eager to join the other animals of the city and to show them that they had the crystal. Their first stop, therefore, would be the Cougar Club Coffee Shop, where the greatest number of animals would be. There, they could also get something to eat.

Brian led the way through every short cut he knew until, at last, the group arrived at its destination. Lit by warm, glowing streetlights and smelling of various types of cuisine favored by the cats, the Coffee Shop was a welcome sight.

The alley was filled with cats that night, but the mood was very somber. There was no music, no dancing, and not much talking. The heroic animals marched in triumphantly, most of them still carrying their swords. Softy clung securely to Licorice's shoulder, just to make sure he wasn't mistaken for a common rodent to be served as an after-dinner treat by the cats.

"It's them!" someone shouted.

A number of cheers arose from the crowd as more cats saw them. Then the whole alley erupted with clapping, cheering, and whistling. All the cats gathered around the group of heroes, shook their paws, patted their backs, and congratulated them. Some of the cats present were the ones who had been freed from Dog Castle earlier that day, and they had spread word about the army of animals. They heartily expressed their thanks, since they never had a good chance to show all their gratitude back at Dog Castle.

Room was made at one table for the entire group, and the chef and his staff prepared a grand feast for the hungry cats, dog, rabbit, and even for Softy. As the group began to eat, the chef asked them to tell the story of their adventure. All of the animals helped tell the tale of their escape from Dog Castle and the recovery of the crystal to a spellbound crowd of cats.

After that, a typical night at the Cougar Club Coffee Shop turned into the biggest party ever in the alley. There was music, dancing, and jubilation the likes of which the animals had never experienced before. Word traveled throughout the city, and gradually cats—and dogs—from all over town stopped by. For the first time in years, the animals rejoiced together. The heroes who had brought back the crystal got to retell the tales from their adventure many times over, and every time they told it they remembered something more.

Around 1:00 A.M., a group of three cats entered the alley. Making their way through the noisy crowd, they seemed to be looking for someone. One of them asked the chef for directions, and he pointed to the table where Tag, Licorice, and Johnny were sitting. The three cats headed in that direction.

Johnny was the first to see the cats approaching, and he could not believe his eyes. At a loss for words, he began tapping Tag and Licorice on their shoulders, but the two brothers were too busy talking to Mandy, Mary, April, and some of their friends. Still speechless, Johnny began shaking them. "Umm…," he stammered.

"What is it?" Tag finally said, turning. Then he saw the three cats. "Oh my gosh…"

Licorice looked then, too, but words were not coming to him either.

One of the three visitors was the old cat who had previously told all the cats about the crystal. The other two cats were Ralph and Daisy!

Tag and Licorice leaped from the table and ran toward their parents. They all embraced. Then Johnny approached and hugged Ralph and Daisy as well. Those two cats looked a little bit older, but not as much older as Tag, Licorice, and Johnny looked to the two parents.

"How did you get here?" asked Tag gleefully.

"We went looking for you," answered Daisy, "after you were taken by the animal catcher. It's a long story, but eventually we ended up here."

"We just got here last night though," added Ralph, "and you had already left."

Tag introduced Softy, Mandy, Mary, and April, who had just walked over there, to their parents. Then Daisy introduced the older cat, with whom most in the group were already acquainted.

"This is my father," Daisy announced proudly. "His name is Julius."

Tag and Licorice were surprised for a second, but then it all made sense. Julius was the cat the condor had met—the older cat, who had told them so much about the crystal, was the one who had hidden it. He was also their grandfather.

"But why didn't you say you were the cat who hid the crystal?" questioned Tag.

"I didn't want word to get around," explained Julius. "It would have been easier for King Wolf to find me."

"Well, we found *this*," Licorice said, handing his grandfather the crystal.

Julius held the crystal and looked it over with familiarity. "I always knew it would come back to me someday," he said pensively, "but I never thought my *grand-kittens* would be the ones bringing it to me!" With that, he gave Tag and Licorice a funny look, and the two brothers could not help laughing.

While the others were having a family reunion, Johnny realized that now was as good a time as any to ask Julius his question.

"I was wondering about something…," he began. "When we were on the mountain…and I caught the crystal when it fell…I found out that *I* was *also* related to the cat who hid the crystal…How can that be?"

Tag and Licorice were surprised again, but they knew there had to be a good explanation—everything they had gone through had happened to Johnny right along with them.

Julius answered him simply. "Well, I had two daughters, Daisy and Rosie. I never saw Rosie after we left the Animals' Forest, but if Rosie had a kitten, he would be just as much my grandson as Tag and Licorice…"

"You mean…," Johnny began.

"I must be *your* grandfather, too," said Julius, "which makes Daisy and Ralph your aunt and uncle…"

At the same moment, Tag, Licorice, and Johnny realized what it all meant.

Johnny turned to Tag and Licorice. "And you guys are my cousins!" he exclaimed joyfully.

The crystal did indeed have an effect on the city as Julius had once predicted. In just the few hours that had already passed, the animals already noticed that there were no people anywhere near them. By all accounts, there were none within miles. For whatever reasons that seemed perfectly normal to them, they had all gotten in their cars, climbed aboard buses or trains, or just started walking, heading…elsewhere.

With the crystal present, the animals' abilities were increased as if they were in the Animals' Forest. They danced and sang like they had never done before, but at the same time, they knew it couldn't last. These were exactly the conditions King Wolf needed to invade the city—once he got himself down from the mountain. Furthermore, the animals knew it wasn't right to deprive the people of their homes in the city. For both of these reasons, the animals knew they had to figure out what to do with the crystal now that it had been brought back. Even while the party had been going on, some of the elder animals who had once lived in the Forest had begun discussing the situation, and by the wee hours of the morning, there was only one acceptable idea.

It was agreed that morning that the animals of the city needed to return and reestablish the old kingdom in the Animals' Forest. As Julius himself pointed out, hiding the crystal again would work no better than it had the first time. Running away from the city was just as pointless. The crystal belonged in the Forest, and that was the only way it could be kept safe from the likes of King Wolf. Though the animals had been unable to defend their kingdom in the past, Julius's grandsons and their friends had proven that the animals *could* protect the crystal, if they had to. This time the kingdom would be better prepared, and the rift that had formed between the cats and dogs would have to come to an end. Everyone knew that the cats and dogs would be much stronger if they stood together, rather than apart. Someone would always be after the crystal, the animals knew, and they just had to be stronger.

Upon hearing the plan, most animals agreed that it was the right decision. Years ago, their community had been disrupted and they had been sent fleeing to Suburb City and beyond, but the Forest was still their true home. There they had the opportunity to build their own society. Instead of trying to avoid the Forest's magic, it was time to embrace it.

Following the party, there was no time to rest for the animals who had brought back the crystal. Julius, Ralph, Daisy, and some of the older dogs and cats went ahead that morning to the Animals' Forest in order to get the crystal out of the city and to start getting things at the kingdom ready; but Tag, Licorice, Johnny, and their friends had an important job to do first. Because of the respect and recognition they had earned, their influence was needed to persuade other animals to join them in the plan to restore the old kingdom. For the whole day, they and others traveled throughout the town to spread the word.

That night, after a busy day and having been up the whole night before, the animals finally got a few precious hours of sleep. Harie and Guarddog stayed with the rich cats at their mansion, but they all knew it would be their last night there.

By noon the following day, it was time to leave. Word had been spread to all corners of the city, and throughout the morning, hundreds of animals had assembled in front of the rich cats' mansion. The staff from the Cougar Club Coffee Shop was on hand, and even Tiger, Toger, and Tugger were there, ready for the trip. Some of the animals were eager to live in the Forest because they wanted to experience its magic. Many more were reluctant because of the past difficulty with the Canine Order, but knowing that there would be many other animals—and the crystal—they had been convinced. Others simply wanted to join Tag, Licorice, and Johnny, who had lately come to be known as the "crystal cats."

In the short time since the crystal had been taken out of the city, many people had returned to their homes and things were nearly back to normal. The animals had spent the morning determining who would carry which of all the various supplies that needed to be brought. Some animals had been given the task of using Tag, Licorice, and Johnny's money—which they were glad to donate—to purchase items they needed. Also, the cash itself needed to be transported, as the animals would need it in the future to purchase more supplies.

As the caravan of animals headed out with some of the elder animals in the lead, Tag, Licorice, and Johnny stood on the sidewalk and said a silent, fond farewell to their old home. They had enjoyed living in a mansion and being the "rich cats" and being famous throughout the city, but that had all been leading up to something even greater. They had already experienced the Forest's effects for a short time, and they knew that, perhaps more than anyone else, that was where they belonged. A new life beckoned them now, but they would not forget the old lady and the good times in the mansion and the city.

Suddenly, they each felt someone's gentle paw on their shoulder. Turning, they saw their cherished girlfriends, Mandy, Mary, and April, and they knew it was time to go.

Tag, Licorice, and Johnny started walking with their girlfriends. After all they had been through together…one day, they knew, they would marry them.

Before they knew it, they were surrounded by all their friends, new and old. Harie, Guarddog, Brian, Ben, Richard, Blackey, and Whitey were all there, weighted down with supplies, ready for whatever adventure lay ahead of them. Softy contentedly climbed atop Licorice's shoulder.

None of the city's people, some of whom had just returned from unexpected business or spontaneous vacations, dared approach such a large group of animals. They just watched with wonder as the massive procession headed down the street. Some were sorry to see their pets leaving them, but somehow they knew that it was right. From the second-story window of one particular house, Penny Wistingsly and her parents watched the parade of animals. They knew their cats were somewhere in that group, and they knew they were okay.

By midnight that evening, all the animals had settled down for a well-earned rest in their new homes within the kingdom in the Animals' Forest. Licorice, however, lay wide-awake in his new room within the central castle. Carefully, he got up from his bed, trying not to awaken anyone. He silently tiptoed down the hall and slipped out into the cool night.

Tag and Johnny were already there, standing on their hind legs, looking over the castle's balcony. He walked up and stood between them.

The past two days had been quite hectic, and there had not been much time to think. Looking back on it now, the three cats knew they had been destined to find the crystal. It was no coincidence at all that Tag and Licorice had met their cousin Johnny. Everything that had happened to them—coming to Suburb City, becoming the "rich cats," and facing the Canine Order—had been part of the crystal's magic. Apart from any of the other animals, their lives had been unique because they were related to the one animal who had first been attracted to that mystical object. Now that they were here, though, in the Animals' Forest, they knew that their remarkable journey was complete. The extraordinary types of events that had brought them to this point would not happen anymore.

Would their lives be dull now? They didn't think so. Living in the Animals' Forest, they would be able to accomplish things that no animal had ever dreamed of. The only difference from before was that whatever happened now would be entirely up to them.

Without saying a word, the three cats peered into the dark woods and the night sky brimming with stars. Together, they looked out into the future and imagined the possibilities…

Made in United States
Orlando, FL
11 May 2023

33063072R00104